Through The Eyes
Of My Mulatto Daughter

Michele L. Waters

Also by Michele L. Waters

Can't Let Go

Reviews,

Can't Let Go,
There are issues that come from dealing with relationships and the
drama of divorce. CAN'T LET GO was able to hold my attention from
the very first sentence.
-Rawsistaz Reviewers

Can't Let Go,
This is an exciting story of real life drama. Michele Waters is
definitely on her way to making her mark in the literary world.
-Cameron Cathey of CSI, NY

Michele L. Waters

Through The Eyes
Of My Mulatto Daughter

Crystall Clear Publishing
www.crystallclearpublishing.com

Through The Eyes of My Mulatto Daughter
Crystall Clear Publishing
ISBN: 978-0-9828670-0-6

© 2010 by Michele L. Waters

Crystall Clear Publishing
25379 Wayne Pl Suite # 193
Valencia, CA. 91355
www.cystallclearpublishing.com
www.michelelwaters.com
Book Cover design by:

Image of Perfection: www.imageofperfection.com
Marion Designs: www.mariondesgns.com
Author Photo by Foxx Studios

Acknowledgments

I would like to take this time to thank all of the authors I have met while traveling around to the many book festivals. The following authors have encouraged and inspired me each and every time I came in contact with them. Pamela Samuels Young, full of knowledge and always sharing. Charles Chatmon, you're a great resource – thanks for looking out for the newbie. Martha Tucker – your dedication to new authors is remarkable. Roland Jefferson, thanks for the tips on low budgeting marketing and the encouraging words. Nicola C. Mitchell, thanks for the tips and sharing resources. To all of the other authors that I have met and shared ideas with but not mentioned by name here, I truly appreciate our conversations. Thank you.

Now for my family and friends that continue to encourage, support and motivate me. Ontresicia Averette, Michele Baham, Denice Bolden, Gretchen Burrell, Chrystal Cohen, Joey Fennel, Margo French, Sabrina Hayes, Denise Janisse, Valencia Marlowe, LaCresha McGuire, Terri J. Preston, Nikki Scott-Richards, Jon Scott, Tracie Todd, Jhinezka Watson, LaFawnda Watson, and Debora Wilson.

Big thanks to all of the Book Clubs that have supported me.

Dedication

For the abused women and children from all walks of life.
Never give up on your dreams.

Be anxious for nothing, but in everything by prayer and supplication, with thanksgiving let your requests be made known to God, and the peace of God, which surpasses all understanding, will guard your hearts and minds through Christ Jesus.

Philippians4:6-7

Chapter One

"Ms. Adams, I'm so sorry we have to do this, but I need you to tell me if this is your father." Detective Henson asked me while holding back the bloody canvas revealing only his face.

I felt numb, like someone had ripped my insides out, then relieved my mother wasn't the one lying beneath the blanket. "Yes. It's him." I finally managed to force the words out.

Detective Henson escorted me out of the room but stopped in the middle of the hallway. "I need to get some information from you. The neighbor called the police after hearing a gunshot. We also got a nine-one-one call from this house, presumably from your mother, saying her husband had been shot. When I knocked on the door to question your mother, she let me in, sat on the sofa, and has been there since but hasn't spoken to anyone." The overstuffed detective paused as he waited for me to fill in the missing pieces that I obviously didn't have. "I hope you understand the seriousness of this."

I nodded yes, but his tone totally confused me. I provided him with the information he requested: my phone number and address. "Can I take my mother home with me now?"

"Sorry, we need to take your mother to the police station. While there's no evidence of a burglary or forced entry, we believe your mother knows what happened. It appears a domestic situation occurred and your mother may have shot your father."

My legs turned into spaghetti noodles. Could my mother have done such a thing? Why was she so quiet? My thoughts were to protect her at all costs. Deep in my heart, I knew she couldn't and wouldn't kill anyone, especially my father. For some reason, she loved him unconditionally. If she was guilty of this, it was an accident. I didn't want to hear the gory details that night; I just wanted to get my mother out of that house, something I'd wanted to do for years.

Marilyn Adams, my mom, was a tall, thin beautiful woman with a silky-smooth coffee hue which turned the heads of most men and women. She was educated, sophisticated, and filled with a sweet southern charm. Her parents, Wilbert and Lillian Halston, my grandparents, were very active in the Civil Rights Movement. Living in the midst of

the movement in Selma, Alabama, in the mid 1960s, danger faced them on a daily basis, but they never backed down. My grandparents weren't sharecroppers; they owned their land and had their own grocery store. During the early to mid sixties white store owners denied blacks credit if they suspected or knew they'd been involved with the Civil Rights Movement. My mom watched her parents open their hearts to many by providing them with food and supplies they needed to make it through the difficult times. They taught their children to never be afraid to fight for what they believed in or for what they wanted in life and to always dream big. God made us all equal, regardless of what the white man said.

My father, Richard Adams, was a very handsome man. Dark hair, deep dark eyes, thick long lashes with chiseled broad bone structure. His build resembled a young Charlton Heston. His parents, I can't call them my grandparents because I always felt tolerated by them, not loved, taught my father and his siblings whites were superior to blacks. Grandpa Adams believed whites and blacks should stay separate in all aspects of life. The two races should never mix. If he had his way, he'd never interact with blacks, not even do business with the "niggers," as he routinely referred to us.

My Grandpa Adams didn't hide the fact he hated my mother. Not even when I was around, which was seldom. My dad always stood up for my mom; defending her against anyone. He fought with Grandpa Adams all the time. Dad was different from his siblings. He loved us. He was my hero – that is, when I was young. Over the years, something happened to that undying love he had for her. At least

3

in my eyes it did. Dad began degrading her, treating her as if she were a second-class citizen. Or worse, as if she were his personal property. I can't pinpoint exactly when this behavior started or when I noticed it, but as I got older, I came to despise my father. I no longer viewed him as my hero but as the same white racist monster his father was. I wanted my mom to leave him so she could be happy again.

Now I'm standing here over his dead body, and I don't know if I want to cry or go out and celebrate.

"Look, as you already know, my father is...was the lieutenant at the Compton Station. If you talk to them, you'll know my mother couldn't have done this. They all know us. They've known us for over thirty years."

"Ma'am, I'm sorry, but I cannot let your mother go until we've finished our investigation."

Detective Henson was a tall rotund middle-aged man, fitting the stereotype of the typical donut-eating policeman. I knew if I were in trouble, I wouldn't want him to be on duty. "Detective, if my mother can tell you what happened, can she come home with me then? I know my mother didn't kill my father. She's not capable of such a violent act. Besides, she loved him. She is definitely in shock. As a matter of fact, she should be taken to the hospital to be checked out."

Detective Henson scratched his thinning receding hairline. Then he flipped open a clean sheet on his notepad.

"It depends on her statement. We need to know what happened." He appeared already convinced she'd committed this heinous crime.

I walked back into the living room, joining my mother on the flower-printed hunter green sofa to question her. Henson followed closely, hoping to be a witness to a confession. She was only fifty-seven, but she looked to be every bit of seventy tonight. She'd lost a lot of weight in the past several months, more than likely from the stress I'd caused her. Just as I was about to ask my mother the question, chills swept through my body, heat rushed to my face, the hairs stood up on the back of my neck. I knew with all of my being she was hiding something. Her eyes were filled with fear, but not regret. I decided at that moment not to question her in front of the detective.

"Mom, you have to go down to the police station. They need to question you about what happened, but I'm going to call a lawyer. I want you to wait and talk to him first. Okay? Do you understand?" She nodded yes and stood up and held her hands towards Henson as a sign to be hand-cuffed. Tears stained her sunken cheeks. I had just recently glimpsed a ray of hope and happiness in my mother the day before. I began to cry as I wrapped my arms around her.

"Did you kill your husband, Mrs. Adams?" My mom continued to cry and never answered. Henson turned to me. "If you know anything about this, you need to tell us. If your mom has nothing to hide, she can just come down to the station for questioning. If she doesn't deny killing your father, I have to assume she did." The detective read my mother her Miranda Rights, handcuffed her, and escorted her to the police car. I followed them out to the car, sobbing while watching them place my mother in the back of a police car like a common criminal and wondering, how did we get here?

Chapter Two

The past year was very unusual for us. My father was the sweetest, most thoughtful, but meanest, man I'd ever known. He was verbally abusive towards my mother. Most of the time he treated her like his personal slave rather than his wife. Maybe he just couldn't help it because it was in his blood. I can't remember any happy moments with my Grandpa Adams. He was even mean to the people he supposedly cared for. I remembered the vile racist comments constantly spewing from his mouth. His hatred for my mother was undeniably the driving force that kept my father away from his family when he found out his mother was dying. Although she wasn't as bad as Grandpa Adams, she was just as cruel. Not seeing his mother on her dying bed haunted my father for years.

Even as a small child, I could feel the evil Grandpa Adams possessed. When I was about eight years old, we had to go back to Alabama for my grandmother's funeral. When my dad, mom, and I walked hand in hand up the crackling wooden steps of the small white church in Selma right off a dirt road from main Highway 80, my grandfather met us at the faintly dull brown painted door. "Why'd ya have to bring them here? Ain't you got no respect for your dead momma, boy?"

My mom clutched my hand, pulling me behind her. She placed her hands over my ears to protect me, so I wouldn't see the monster they called my grandpa but it didn't work. I had heard the foul comments. Even worse, I'd seen the wickedness in his eyes and the fear in hers.

My father squalled out, "This is my family, whether you like it or not . We're not goin' anywhere!" He appeared to be trying to not draw any attention from the other mourners.

"I can't believe you'd bring this black wench in here and disgrace your momma like this." Black wench? Disgrace? I couldn't recall these words in any books I'd read or any spelling words I'd reviewed in school, so I couldn't figure out the exact meaning at the time. I knew they weren't compliments of any kind. I remembered an intense feeling watching all of those white people staring at us – looking like they were feening for a lynching. I remembered learning about lynchings during Black History month later in school. Many southern whites watched, mainly black men being hung, burned, and sometimes other forms of torture as a form of entertainment. Mom looked frightened. Her grip tightened on my hand. I looked up at her and wanted to let her know everything would be all right. At that time, I thought my father would surely protect her from any danger. He was the police. He had a gun and a badge. No one would ever hurt his family. I always felt safe around Dad, and Mom was no pushover. This was a different brand of people...a different kind of white people than I was used to.

Mom really stood out because she was brown skinned – not too dark, but definitely darker than a brown paper bag. I was what they considered "passing" back then so my father probably could have eased me in with no fuss. Thinking back, I'm pretty sure that was the only reason my grandparents tolerated me when I hung out with my dad whenever we were in Alabama. We went back there often to see my mother's parents. They were the nicer grandparents. They were the ones that smothered me with hugs and kisses everyday we were there and were sad to see us leave.

That night, my dad and I went to Grandpa Adams' house to say good-bye. Mom stayed behind at her parents' house. When we got there, I was told to go into a room to watch T.V. while my dad stayed in the kitchen talking to my grandfather. The house was small. There was a living room at the front of the house with a door to the right that led to the kitchen. To the left was a narrow hallway that led to two bedrooms and a bathroom. There were heaters or radiators on the floor. I remembered them yelling at each other a lot and my grandfather telling my dad he had made the biggest mistake in his life by marrying "that woman." That's how he referred to my mom. I tried to tune out the shouting by turning the small black and white television up. Those were the only real memories I had of my grandfather, Herbert Adams.

"Hi, Dad, where's Mom?" I used my usual respectful but cold tone. Dad refused to have a sprinkler system installed for the yard. He stood on the richly green lawn spraying a stream of water over his perfectly manicured yard. He swung the water hose aside so I could walk up to him without getting wet.

"Hey, Princess, come give your old man a hug." I gave him a weak hug. "Your mom's in the house washing or something."

"Okay." I walked away quickly so he couldn't engage me in trivial conversation. "Mom, Mom?" There was no answer. I tiptoed through the house so I could sneak up on her and startle her. I don't know why I always got a kick out of seeing her jump. Dad had her jumpy enough. I don't know why she got a kick out of me scaring her just as much as I did. Their house was stuck in the early eighties. The kitchen sported blue laminate countertops with a dingy vinyl floor. Walking into each room was like taking a time machine back two decades. Light blue carpet was laid throughout the entire house. The house was a moderate sized home – four bedrooms, two bathrooms, a huge kitchen, a formal dining room, a family room, and a living room. The house was very boxy, not an open floor plan. All of the common living areas were cut off from each other. I stopped calling out for Mom because I became more nosy than playful. I wanted to see what had her so distracted she couldn't hear her "Princess" calling her. I spotted a light shining from the closet of one of the guest bedrooms. While moving towards the light, I could hear the rustling of papers. I peeped into the small walk-in closet and noticed my mother on the floor looking at old photos. A shoebox sat in front of her filled with more photos. "Mom?" The sound of my voice startled her. "What are you doing?" I kneeled down beside her and noticed she had tears in her eyes. She clenched two photos in her hands.

"Nothing." She was defensive and then her demeanor changed suddenly with a huge smile as she wrapped her arms around me. "How are you, sweetie? I didn't know you were coming by this evening."

"I'm fine, but what are you doing in here and who are these pictures of?"

"Please don't ask." Before I could ask again, we heard the kitchen door slam. We both jumped. Mom quickly placed the pictures back in the shoebox, hid it behind a large organizer storage box, and pushed it under huge thick comforters. She turned to me, placing her index finger to her lips and motioning me to be quiet. Mom grabbed my hand, pulling me out of the closet, turned the lights out, and practically dragged me to the kitchen. Dad had planted himself at the sink, polishing off a tall glass of ice water. Although we were not itty bitty women, Dad made us look dainty in comparison to his thick six foot three inch frame.

"Brittney, have you had a chance to call James yet?" My father had been trying to set me up with some young hot-headed detective who recently transferred to his station.

"I told you I'm not interested in him. Why are you pushing him on me? Is it because he's white?"

"Look, I told you before it has nothing to do with that. I just want you to have a good man, one who will take care of you."

"Oh, like you take care of mom? No thanks. What makes you think he's such a good man? You barely know him. Since he's white, he must be all right. Is that it?" I was always in defense mode when entering my parents' home.

"Please, can't we have one night without it becoming a racial argument?" Mom pleaded.

"I don't know where she gets this nonsense from. I'm married to a black woman, or did you forget that?"

"No, how could anyone forget it? You remind us of it all the time as if you're some great humanitarian for marrying the poor helpless black woman."

"Please, Brittney, don't do this." Although Mom was a tall woman, she looked small and feeble. I knew my heated arguments with my father taxed her. I had become livid with how my father treated my mother. I hadn't witnessed any physical abuse, but he verbally attacked her daily. I pleaded with my mother on several occasions to leave him and live with me, but she didn't think he was so bad. He provided for her. She told me she never wanted for anything. Was this all marriage was supposed to be? I thought. Had she become complacent with the constant disrespect she faced every day? I believed after thirty-six years, she'd become immune to it.

"Mom, I'll talk to you later." I gave her a peck on her cheek and turned towards the door to leave, when my father grabbed me so hard I thought he might have yanked my shoulder out of its socket.

"Don't hurt her!" There was that same fear in my mother's eyes I had only seen once as a child. She was petrified my father would or could really hurt me. Why would she believe he was capable of physically hurting me?

"Get your hands off of me! I'm not Mom. If you ever put your hands on me again, I'll have you arrested!" I jabbed my finger at his face.

"Who do you think is going to come out here and arrest the lieutenant of the sheriff's department? Look, girl, I've tolerated your disrespect and sassiness long enough. I'm warning you, stop this absurd talk now." He had an arrogant, pompous attitude.

I had always been the light of my parents' life, my father's little Princess. He had always been so proud of me. He attended every extra-curricular activity I was in. As I got older, I began to realize my father wasn't that nice to my mother, and as I became a teenager, it seemed to bother me more and more to hear my father treat my mother so mean. He tried to not be too awful in front of me, but I heard little demeaning remarks all the time. After I returned home from college, the subtle disrespectful comments towards my mother had turned into blatant verbal abuse. That's when my relationship with my father changed drastically. The abuse had always been there, but when I left for college, something changed. It became more prevalent. That's also around the time Grandpa Adams died. The older I got, the more verbal I became in defense of my mother since she didn't see the need to defend herself. "I'll talk to you tomorrow, Mom." I left and went home.

The next morning, I went to work. I had a new client coming in, a sixteen-years-old-and-four-months pregnant teenager. Angela Johnson was due to check into The Ebony Eyes Residence for unwed mothers around nine o'clock. Mary Cooper, the caregiver, finished the check-in process documenting all of her items before she brought her to my office. Angela walked in glaring at all of the photos and accolades that surrounded my small office. My L-shaped desk sat in the middle of the room with black shelving circling the entire room. There, I had photos of all the young women Ebony Eyes Residence had helped through-out the years. I was very proud of our accomplishments for providing a much needed service for young pregnant teens. We also worked with different programs at some of the local schools to provide living assistance training for everything from learning to diaper a baby to preparing for job interviews. This home was my heart.

"Hello, Angela, welcome to The Ebony Eyes Residence." I stood up and extended my hand. She shook my hand and sat in the chair across from my desk. Angela's mother had decided to have her placed in the home because she had two other children and was tired of the disciplinary problems that persisted daily with Angela.

"Hi, are we allowed to have company here?" This child was kicked out of her home and in a few months would be giving birth to a baby, and all she was concerned with was having company?

13

"Of course. However, there's a curfew and a visitor's policy which is strictly enforced. As a matter of fact, why don't we go over all of the rules now?" I explained the policies and procedures to Angela and gave her a tour of the premises. The house was a huge two-story with five bedrooms and four baths. We were licensed for up to eight girls, but I usually kept only five, sometimes six if there was no other home available. Girls are a handful, especially when teenage hormones meet pregnancy hormones. I prided our home in providing one-on-one assistance as much as possible.

It was an unusually turbulent day. Seemed everyone in the home had boyfriend drama. One of the resident's boyfriend had been giving too much attention to one of the other girls in the home. Things got heated between the two girls. I knew they were young women, but I couldn't bring myself to refer to them as such. They were very childlike, not having a clue of the importance of keeping themselves safe for the sake of their unborn child. Maria, a feisty Puerto Rican, was eight months pregnant. That didn't stop her from slapping the crap out of Sandra, a thick white girl straight out of the hood, when she saw her cozying up to her "man." Thank God I had Amazon-built women caring for these girls. They had the situation under control before I could even dial nine-one-one.

With all the drama going on in the home, I still couldn't shake the thoughts of my visit to my parents' house the night before. I wondered; what was my mom hiding? Who were those people in the photos? My mom was the most dedicated, loyal, committed wife I'd ever known. I couldn't believe she hid secrets from my father.

I finished my incident reports and progress notes for the day and made sure the schedules were complete for the weekend activities. I was anxious to get home tonight. It was the first Friday in months I didn't have an event planned. My event planning business was getting busier and busier. Soon I would need to make a choice between the two loves of my life. I called Mom to let her know I'd be coming over. I knew tonight we'd be alone. Dad hung out with his police buddies every Friday night. Most of the guys my father seemed to gravitate towards had the same mentality – egotistical, prejudiced, chauvinistic, bigoted, dogmatic, and narrow-minded. Birds of a feather definitely flocked together.

Chapter Three

When I arrived at the house, Mom appeared timid and anxious, which was normal for her on Fridays. After a night of getting wasted with the boys, Dad's personality was usually on an entirely different level. I'd never personally witnessed my father hitting my mother, but I suspected he had on occasion. Maybe he didn't punch, but I'd almost bet my life savings he did something physical. There wasn't a woman who'd be so skittish from only verbal abuse.

"Hey, Mom."

"Hey, Princess." She hugged me tighter and longer than usual. I could see in her eyes she longed to tell me something. It was time for her to share her secret. Earlier, I suspected this might be a difficult task, but I knew now it'd be quite simple to get the story out of her.

"Mom, we need to talk."

"I know. It's time." We strolled down the hallway hand in hand and then dipped into the guest bedroom. Mom walked hesitantly to the closet door where she held her secret. She slowly pulled the door open, seemingly wondering if she should share her secret with me or not. She kneeled down and scrambled through the storage boxes and clothes and pulled out the shoe box containing the photos I had glanced yesterday. She carried the box to the bed, protecting it as if it were a hidden treasure. We sat side by side but I waited for her to open the box. As she pulled the pictures out, tears filled her eyes.

"Mom, who are these people?" Most of the pictures were of little boys with their parents, but as I closely examined the photos, it looked like the same boy with different family members. I was so confused. Why was Mom so emotional, secretive, and protective of these strangers? I didn't recognize any of these people as our family. Mom pulled out a picture of two newborn babies. I couldn't tell if they were boys, girls, or one of each but they looked just alike, maybe twins.

She stroked her index finger across the picture and the tears began to flow again. "Princess, these boys..." she gazed at me, "are your little brothers." Mom closed her eyes, clutching the pictures close to her chest. What was she talking about? She'd never been pregnant, at least I didn't remember seeing her pregnant. Were these boys a result of my father having an affair? I sat there dumbfounded with my mouth hanging open.

She dropped her head into her hand crying. "Mom, please stop. You have to explain this to me, please. Did dad have an affair?" She stopped crying while shaking her head no.

"I gave birth to them when you were three years old." The tears came flowing again while she began frenetically trying to explain. "Your grandfather, that monster, convinced your father we should give them up at birth."

"I don't understand. Why would he give away his own sons? Were you having financial problems?"

"I prayed they wouldn't be born too dark. I overheard Herbert telling your father it would make his life a living hell if he had to raise a black boy. Herbert told your father not to be fooled by the light complexion at birth, to check the top of the ears to see how dark the child would really be. He told your father not to waste any time getting rid of him."

I thought, okay, she's making no sense. What is she talking about checking the top of ears? I had my issues with my father, but this was even far-fetched for him. I mean, he did have a superiority complex but...men loved bragging about their sons. No matter what...didn't they? "But, Mom, why'd you allow him to do this? Why didn't you leave Dad and go back to Grandma's house?" Mom's parents were like fairytale parents. They were supportive and loved her so much they'd do anything for her and I knew that, so why would she go along with this?

"I told him I'd leave him if he tried to take my baby. He told me if I didn't give the baby away, only if it was a boy, he'd take you away and I would never see you again." She cried.

My father and I bumped heads often because of the way he constantly disrespected my mother, but somehow I still felt he loved her. I would never have imagined he could be so cruel as to threaten to take me away from my mother. What did that say for the love I thought he had for me? I wiped her drenched face. The more she spoke, the more confused I became.

"I couldn't take that chance to lose you. Not my little Princess." She shook her head, sniveling while wiping her face with her sleeve.

"I'm sorry, Mom. I don't understand this. You've lived with the fear of Dad taking me away, but when I finished school, why didn't you leave? Did you ever try to find them? How'd you get these pictures?" Mom swiveled her body towards me, seemingly surprised at all the questions. She attempted to gather herself enough to answer them.

"There was a lady that worked in Social Services who knew I didn't want to give them away. At that time, the rules were the family giving the child away couldn't have any information on the adoptive parents."

"Wait, you've jumped way ahead of me. Tell me of the day you gave birth. What happened that day? How'd they just take your babies without your authorization?"

Mom's body quivered as she took in an exasperated breath and began to recall the day she gave birth to my twin brothers.

"'Push! You have to push hard, Marilyn!' the doctor and nurse told me." She started explaining.

"'I'm pushing as hard as I can, woman!'" My mother seemed to be remembering the exact words of her response as she continued to relive the day of the twins' birth. She seemed to be in a trance-like state, as if she could vividly remember the events of that fateful day....

"'Ok. Here we go. I see the crown. Okay, Marilyn, a couple more times and we'll be finished. On three you need to give it all you've got. One, two, three, push!'"

Mom began rocking from side to side as she continued with the account of her story. She looked like she was reliving the entire event. It was hard seeing her so drained but I had to understand how this had happened.

"'AHHHHH! I screamed," Mom said.

"'Again. okay, we got it.' A baby came out and a nurse quickly wrapped the baby into a sheet. Before she could leave, the doctor said, 'uh- oh.'"

"'What's the problem?'

"'We have another one.'"

"The nurse placed my baby in a little crib and rushed over to the doctor's side. I heard her say, 'Are we going to need to perform a Cesarean?'"

"'Looks like it's turned sideways, but the head's first.'"

"'What's happening? Why aren't you bringing my baby to me? Is it a boy or girl?' The nurse looked at the doctor as if unsure how to answer me."

"The doctor said, 'Marilyn, you have another child. You have twins. You need to push again. Do you understand? Are you still with me?'"

"'Yes.'"

"'Get ready. On three, okay? One, two, three, push!'"

"After about two or three more pushes, another baby came out. Again the nurse grabbed the baby without telling me anything and placed the baby in a sheet. Another nurse came in and they each took a baby out of the room. I remember feeling like I was in a bad nightmare I couldn't wake up from."

"'Doctor, where are they taking my babies?'"

"'Marilyn, based on you and your husband's instructions, they're going directly to the adoption agency.'"

"I was stunned. 'What are you talking about? I didn't instruct anyone to take my babies.' I told them to get my husband right then 'He's a policeman.' I screamed at them, thinking that would get my babies back immediately. 'There's been some kind of mistake. I want my babies!' I screamed and screamed at doctors and nurses, but no one would bring my babies to me. I tried to get off the table, but the doctor and nurse held me down. Next thing I knew, I was floating. The room was spinning and I woke up hours later in a room."

Mom paused and wiped her face, still trembling and shaking her head. She continued her story.

"A nurse came in to check my vitals and asked how I was feeling. I told her I was fine but wanted to see my babies. She said, 'Mrs. Adams, you don't have any babies.' That statement sent me in total panic. I didn't know why, but I couldn't move my body. Minutes later the doctor came in."

"'Marilyn, are you feeling better now?'"

"Where are my babies? Why are you people keeping them from me?"

"'Marilyn, you signed to have your child taken at birth. I spoke to your husband about this on more than one occasion to make sure this is what both of you wanted.' When he told me, I just started crying because I knew your father had done this and it would be impossible to fight him. If I tried to fight it, he'd take you like he'd threatened to do."

"'What did I have? Can you tell me that?' I asked."

"'They were very healthy, beautiful baby boys.' The doctor smiled while my heart was crumbling into a million pieces."

"'Where's my husband?'"

"'He'll be in soon. He's finishing up with some more paperwork. Well, I just wanted to check on you before I left for the evening. Most likely you'll be released tomorrow if there are no complications throughout the night.' He left still smiling like he'd done a great deed for the day."

"Several minutes later Richard walked into the room. My eyes were swollen and red from crying. He sat down in the chair next to the bed and had the audacity to ask, 'Are you all right?'"

"I thought, the nerve of him to come in here so nonchalant after snatching my babies from me. 'How do you think I'm doing? You just stole my children from me. How could you do this to me, to our family?'"

"'Come on, Marilyn, we already discussed this. We both decided it would be best.' Richard said like it was no big deal to give up our own flesh and blood."

"I turned and looked at him. I couldn't believe the lie he was telling. I yelled, 'First, we didn't agree to anything. You threatened to take Brittney from me if I didn't give the baby up – if it was a boy – and if he was too dark. Secondly, we agreed we wouldn't make a decision at the hospital. We'd wait. Instead, you tricked me into signing over my babies without knowing it. How can you claim to love me and do something like this? If you don't fix this and get my babies back, I'll never forgive you for this. Please, Richard, fix this before our babies are gone.' I was in a hysterical panic."

"Richard said, 'The adoptive parents were here during the delivery. They already have one of the babies. Since they were only expecting one, the other one is being sent to the foster care agency. They're on their way here to get him now.' Your father said this like he was talking about new-born pups he'd bred to sell."

"'No!' I cried. I tried to get out of the bed, but my legs were strapped down. That was dumb, I thought. I finally regained the strength to sit up and untied one of the straps. Richard held me down and called for the nurse."

"Two nurses and a man came in. Richard said, 'She's hysterical. I told you this might happen. You need to strap her back down.'"

"I couldn't believe the man I loved was doing this to me. Within seconds, I was strapped down like a patient in a mental asylum. I cried for someone to help me. Everyone only listened to his instructions. While I continued to struggle, I noticed an older black woman with a clipboard standing outside the room, peeking in. She walked in and said, 'What's going on here?'"

"One of the nurses responded, 'Let's go outside so I can explain.' They left together. The other nurse and man followed behind after injecting something into my I.V. line."

My mother's eyes showed a slow, torturous return to the present. As I sat there near her with my mouth wide open in shock, I heard the rest of her painful story.

"A few hours later I woke up again. Richard was asleep in the chair next to me. I guess pretending to be a loving, faithful husband. This time I remained quiet and tried to figure out what was going on. I thought about you. I wanted to see and hold my little girl right then. I remember an overwhelming fear came over me. My heart began pounding rapidly. I realized Richard had made all of the arrangements – even the babysitter. I didn't know where you were. I hadn't made arrangements with our regular sitter to keep you. Everything happened so fast. I thought, who has Brittney? Where was my daughter? My plan changed. My first priority was to get you."

"Two days later I was released. They were the longest two days of my life. Although I'd questioned Richard regarding your whereabouts, he'd been very vague. I never got a straight answer. He held your location over me like a master waving a bone over a hungry dog to make him behave in order to get his treat. When Richard came to pick me up, he brought you in with him. I was so happy to see your sweet innocent face I swore to never let you out of my sight again."

The rage and contempt I felt for my father increased as I watched her revisiting the nightmare she'd endured over thirty years ago. I wanted to feel more empathy for her, but I needed to hear the whole story. Although Mom was indeed the victim, I still couldn't figure out why she didn't leave Dad later. Why didn't she try to find her sons? "Mom, how'd you get these pictures?"

"One day, only weeks after their birth, I went to Social Services. The woman I'd seen when I was in the hospital, Margaret Wilson, saw me wandering around the office and waved at me to come into her office. She was the only one I told about your father's threat. She said I should go to the police, but if he was capable of following through with the threat, I'd be taking a chance on losing my daughter. I asked her to give me the information on the couple. She explained she couldn't but she gave me photos of the babies. She told me she'd ask the adoptive parents to take Jerome also in an attempt to keep them together but couldn't make any promises. About a month later she contacted me. I'd given her your father's work schedule to avoid any problems. She told me the couple decided to keep only the one baby and the other one was in foster care. She made sure he was in a good home."

Mom told me the couple that adopted one of my brothers named him Jaden Patterson. My brother that was placed in the foster home took their last name Roclin, Jerome Roclin. Mom went on to explain what she knew of my brothers Jaden and Jerome. She kept up with everything about them up until the time Ms. Margaret took ill and eventually died. For ten years, Ms. Margaret provided Mom with information about her sons. It had been over twenty years since then. At that time, neither twin knew the other existed, as far as we knew.

Jaden grew up in Southern California. From what Mom was told by Ms. Margaret, the couple never had any other children. At least up to the age of ten, Jaden was an only child.

Jerome also grew up in California, in the Bay Area, but had been through six different foster homes by the time he was ten. While studying the pictures, Mom said Jerome always looked so sad and lonely in the pictures.

Watching her reminisce over the pictures, while sharing what little information she had on my brothers, I became furious with her. "Mom, I'm…grown and have been for a very long time. Why didn't you leave Dad and try to find your sons? Did he threaten to kill you if you left him?" Deep down I hoped he had. That would at least excuse this crackbrained behavior.

"Princess, things were very different back then when your father and I married. It was a different kind of world for interracial couples. Although the laws for interracial couples had changed, society hadn't, especially in the south."

What the hell did that have to do with anything? I felt it coming; Mom was going to give me some long story to make my father seem almost heroic for marrying her. I was getting sick to my stomach with the thought of the direction she'd attempt to take this conversation yet again. I couldn't take it – not now. "Mom, please don't go there."

"No, you have to hear me. I mean, really hear me and understand what I'm telling you. You need to understand the world we lived in. His life and his family's life were truly endangered. He had to leave his family's home because he stood up to all those white racist pigs. His family couldn't take the pressure. They disowned him. One day he was walking home after visiting me and four men started chasing him on Highway Eighty. You know where those railroad tracks are right before you get to your grandma's church?" I rolled my eyes nodding yes. "They caught him and beat him nearly to death. The hospital staff reported the incident to the police, but when they questioned your father, the police said the guys had reported he tried to rob them with a gun. They said they were acting in self-defense. They knew your father. It was a small town. They knew what had really happened but they sided with the thugs who nearly beat him to death."

Mom went on to tell me that in the state of Virginia it was against the law for blacks and whites to marry all the way up to the late 1960s. Even when that law was banned by the Supreme Court in Alabama, the practice remained the same. The white racists feared desegregation would encourage more interracial unions. The hatred and abuse their families encountered as a result of their union forced them to move to California shortly after their marriage. She spoke at length about how life was in the South for her and my father, as though this would excuse his behavior and bring me some sort of peace and acceptance. Instead, it infuriated me even more. How could someone who'd been treated so poorly and discriminated against turn his back on his own flesh and blood because of the color of their skin? How could he allow Grandpa Adams, the man he viewed as a racist, to give him any advice about his own children? That made no sense.

We both jumped when we heard the front door slam.

"Marilyn, I'm home," he slurred.

Mom and I immediately began tossing the pictures back in her secret place. When we finished getting everything covered, she turned to me. "Don't leave until he falls asleep."

Her asking me to stay until my dad fell asleep was a confirmation he hadn't changed in his old age. I obliged her request. We went out to the living room to meet my drunkard father.

"Hey, Princess, I didn't see your car out there. What are you doing here so late? Never mind. Just give your ol' man a hug."

He reeked of liquor. I couldn't stand him before. Now I despised him even more. This man I called Dad was not only mean but evil. Although I continued to agonize over Mom living with this man, now I was more concerned with finding my brothers.

"Do you want some dinner?" Mom asked.

"Did I ask for any dinner?" Dad snarled back at her. "You know you're supposed to have my bath ready for me. Why are you acting so stupid?"

I was sick of being my mother's protector, but tonight I was more than ready to take on that role. "Who in the hell do you think you're talking to like that? She's not your slave." Then I turned to my mother. "Why don't you stand up for yourself for a change? I don't know what's wrong with you. You've allowed him to treat you like you're less than dirt your whole marriage. When are you going to get a spine?"

Mom had a shocked look on her face. I walked out. Something told me not to drive away, but I was so fed up with both of them I ignored my instincts, hopped in my shiny black BMW, turned the volume up and drove away.

Chapter Four

While the information was fresh in my mind, I hurried to my office, grabbed a manila folder from my drawer and started a file for Jaden and Jerome. I wrote everything I'd learned of them so far. I searched the Internet for the hospital Jaden and Jerome were born in and the agency where the social worker, Ms. Margaret, worked before dying. Thank goodness Mom had kept the agency's information along with the pictures,. I could barely wait for Monday so I could gather more information.

Since this was my first Saturday off in months, I'd agreed to have an all day date with Matthew Turner, a parole detective I met months ago at one of the events I'd planned for one of my girlfriends from college. Matthew was a big dark chocolate fine brotha, but I also detected a soft, sweet side. We'd been talking on the phone for months, but scheduling conflicts seemed to keep us apart. We both looked forward to spending the day together. I planned to not think about my brothers or my mother and enjoy the day.

I finished reviewing all the psychiatric and medical reports for the residents at Ebony Eyes and completed my housework in a couple hours. Now I had plenty of time to get cute. "It's been so long. I hope I remember how to act on a date." As I dabbed a bit of perfume behind both ears, I heard the doorbell. I jumped, took another quick glance in the mirror and rushed to meet Matthew. I swung the door open without checking through the peephole.

"Hi."

"Well hello, Ms. Brittney." He took my hand and kissed it as he entered.

I stood there watching and smiling like a high school girl. "So are you ready to hang out?"

"You know, I've been waiting a long time for this day. I see you took my advice and dressed comfortably. We're going to see what you're made of today."

"Sounds good to me. I'm no little sissy. I can hang." I hoped I'd be able to keep the thought of my little brothers out of my mind just for today. I knew I couldn't go the whole day without checking on my mom. I felt guilty walking out on her last night. "Come in and have a seat. I need to make a quick call before we leave."

Although this was a casual date, Matthew looked and smelled so good. He had on jean shorts and a T-shirt with spotless white tennis shoes. He strolled into the family room and plopped on the couch. "The remote is on the coffee table. This will only take about ten minutes."

"Okay, take your time. I'm not going anywhere."

I bolted to my room and closed the door behind me. "Hello, Dad, is Mom around?"

"Yes. You know, every once and a while you could call to talk to your dad. I'm your parent, too, you know."

"I'm in a rush right now. Can I speak to Mom please?"

"Marilyn! Your daughter's on the phone."

"Hello."

"Hi, Mom, are you okay?"

"Of course, why wouldn't I be?" Her tone was soft but very sarcastic. I was tired of trying to protect her, always putting my happiness aside to worry about her. I decided today I'm not doing it. If she says she's fine, then that's what I'm going with. I refuse to feel guilty.

"I just wanted to apologize for storming out on you last night. Are you sure you're all right?"

"Positive. Aren't you supposed to be going on a date today?"

"Yes, Matthew's here. We're leaving in a few minutes. I'll be out all day, so I wanted to check on you before I left."

"Princess, I'm fine. Go out and have a good time. You deserve it."

"Okay. I'll talk to you tomorrow." I felt somewhat relieved after our brief conversation.

I reached for my duffle bag. The plan was to go hiking along a trail somewhere around Griffith Park, then go back to his place to shower and change for our evening date.

We entered into the park off Chrystal Springs Trail and drove through the winding roads until Matthew found the spot he'd picked out to test my athleticism. First thing I noticed was a huge sign that read: Beware of coyotes and rattlesnakes. *Great. I'm coming out here to run with the coyotes and snakes. I'm scared to death of snakes and never even thought of sharing an area with coyotes.* Matthew parked the car in a secluded area. I stepped out hesitantly. We met at the back of his Sequoia, snatched a blanket and cooler and headed to a nearby picnic area. We dropped the items down and jetted for the trail.

We talked as we went up and down hill after hill. The crunching sound of my shoes pounding on the gravel made me sound as if I were a three hundred pound woman. I'm no small fry, just shy of five feet eight inches. I went tramping along the dirt trail like a true Amazon.

After about an hour and a half of this torture, we were almost back to the picnic area. I didn't want to admit it, but my legs felt like they'd betray me at any time by collapsing out from under me. By the time we made it back to our blanket to have lunch, I wanted to pass out right there. But no, Matthew decided we needed to walk another few hundred feet just to find the perfect spot under a huge tree. My mouth was dry, my chest tight. Maybe I was going to have a heart attack, but I was much too stubborn and full of pride to admit it.

"Are you okay? Is this too much for you?" He had a condescending smirk.

"Please. I'm cool. I just should have brought more water." What's one little lie on a first date?

We sat for a couple of hours talking about everything from office politics to relationships. I felt so comfortable talking to him. I thought of divulging the information I'd recently learned about my brothers in hopes of receiving help or advice. Being a parole officer, I was sure he had resources at his fingertips to assist him in getting around the red tape to obtain information on people. I didn't know him well enough to start confessing all of our dirty laundry so soon. Besides, I wasn't sure if I wanted him to know I'd been raised by such a weak mother. Anxiety swept through my body as I sat thinking about what Mom had revealed to me. What kind of monster had raised me? What kind of blood ran through my veins?

"Hey, you still with me?" Matthew tapped me on my leg.

"Huh? Oh yeah. Sure I am. Just enjoying the beautiful sunshine." Okay, that was lie number two. "So what else is on the agenda for today?"

"We'll go back to my house, take showers and then we're off to the Film Festival for a special viewing of an independent film produced by a good friend of mine."

"Producer friend, oh so you have those kinds of friends. I might be just a little impressed." I smiled while pinching my thumb and index finger together inches from his face.

"Well, let's see it first before either of us are impressed."

We packed up everything we'd brought for our picnic, trekked back to the car and were inside his house within thirty minutes. We showered and changed into our evening clothes and made it to Westwood Village just in time for the first showing. It turned out his friend, Eddie Washington, had produced a great documentary exposing the government's role in the economic meltdown. Everything was explained in layman's terms; a sixth grader could understand how the middle man had gotten totally screwed.

"The documentary hit on exactly what we were discussing earlier," he said.

I knew Matthew was talking but I couldn't hear him. I was shocked at what I was witnessing. There was a man barking at a meek looking woman in front of a crowd. Almost as if he was doing it to get attention from his buddies. She stood there unquestionably humiliated but stood there as if her feet were planted into the cement.

"Hello? Brittney? What are you staring at?" Matthew turned and noticed the group of people. "Oh yeah, he's a big macho man, picking on that helpless woman. I'm sure his persona is bigger than his bravo."

I snapped back. "Huh? What did you say?"

"Men like that kill me. Actually they're kinda funny. He's a scared little boy inside but wears the mask of a tough guy. If he used that mask with men they'd punch his lights out, so he uses it on women because it's safer. He's the worst kind of coward."

"That mask only works on certain types of women," I said boastfully.

"Of course. Most of them know what kind of women they're safe with and those are the ones they prey on."

"I know him."

"You do?" Matthew seemed stunned.

I laughed. "My father introduced me to him. He wanted me to go out with him." Before Matthew could comment, I heard my name being called. I looked around and James was making his way towards us faster than a runaway freight train.

"Hey, Brittney." James smiled innocently, probably hoping I hadn't observed his outrageous chauvinistic behavior.

"Hello, James, how are you?"

"I'm great. What's going on?" He spied Matthew.

I could tell he was dying to know who this gorgeous man standing next to me was so I obliged. "Nothing much. Just enjoying the festival. This is Matthew Turner and this is..." I turned towards James. I wanted to say the jackass my father wanted me to go out with, but I held my tongue... "James."

Matthew shook his hand. "What's up?" Matthew gave him a look as if he were daring him to step out of line.

"What's up man? Don't I know you?" I could tell James knew he had to keep his tough guy facade. After all, he was a detective.

"I don't think we've ever met."

"Well, I never forget a face. I'm sure it'll come to me."

Then the two exchanged cold stares. I thought I'd better break this up before we had a battle of the egos. "Well maybe you two have seen each other in passing. Matthew's a parole officer." I glanced at James. "James is a detective." I winked at Matthew.

"Perhaps I've seen you at the station." James had a half crooked smile.

"That could be it." Matthew still watched him as if to say he didn't care what he did for a living.

"So how's the lieutenant?" James asked.

"You tell me. You probably see him more than I do."

The young lady that had been ripped publicly by James had eased her way over to us but he'd engaged in some small talk about the festival with Matthew and didn't acknowledge her presence so I did. "Hi, I'm Brittney and this is Matthew."

"Oh yeah, this is Sandie," James said shyly and then immediately focused on me. "So when are we going to get together?" I guess he forgot Matthew and Sandie were standing right next to us.

"Excuse me?"

"Your father said you were interested in taking shooting lessons."

Before I could speak, Matthew said, "Actually, we got that under control. I'll be taking her to the range and teaching her everything she needs to know about shooting a gun."

"I guess the lieutenant doesn't know about this arrangement. He didn't mention it to me. I just saw him yesterday."

I laughed, "Well, my father doesn't know everything about me, nor does he schedule my play dates."

"Of course not," James muttered shamefully. "Well, I'll see you around. You two have a nice evening."

"You do the same," Matthew said.

As he walked away, Sandie leaned towards him whispering something, probably making it known she hadn't appreciated his obvious flirtations towards me in front of her. He blurted out, "Shut the hell up!"

Matthew looked at me. "How well does your father know this guy he's trying to hook you up with? From what I've learned about you so far, I can't see you with him."

"Neither can I. If you ever see me with him, you'll know someone must have drugged, hypnotized or brainwashed me. So come to my rescue and save me." We both laughed.

Chapter Five

I got up bright and early and worked most of the morning because I had to make up for being away all day yesterday with Matthew. There was always some business to take care of between planning events and running Ebony Eyes. I decided to visit Mom but I knew I wouldn't have a chance to talk to her about my brothers because Dad would be there.

Just as I was about to leave, I received a call from Ebony Eyes. Two of the young ladies were at it again over some man. What was wrong with our young girls these days?

Within thirty minutes I stepped to the front door embarrassed from the words I heard from the screaming teens inside.

The weekend manager, Ms. Wilma, and the other weekend staffer, Dinora, were scuffling to keep Ninette and Cherokee apart. I noticed the chairs were positioned in a circle. When the girls had issues with each other, one of the recommendations from our behavior therapist was to have the ladies involved sit down in a calm manner along with a staff member to discuss and come up with solutions to fix the problem. Hearing the screaming coming from the house, I could see this was premature of the staff to think these two were ready for a calm sit down rap session.

I was not in the mood to deal with this teenage drama and I guessed the look on my face expressed that because when the teens saw me, they immediately changed their tone and sat in the chairs, facing each other.

"What's going on?" Neither of the teens spoke.

Dinora finally said, "They're fighting again over some no-good man. I told them they both need to leave his trifling butt alone."

I watched Dinora wondering is she really staff or is she a resident? Sometimes I couldn't tell the difference. I attempted to ignore her but she didn't get the hint.

"Go head, Cherokee. Tell Ms. Adams what you guys were fighting about," Dinora continued.

Before she could utter another word, I said, "Dinora, can you go into the kitchen and help the others start preparing lunch? Ms. Wilma and I will handle things in here." Ms. Wilma looked at me, rolling her eyes. I knew she was mentally worn out having to monitor the staff as much as the immature pregnant teens.

Dinora yelled out, "Ladies, wash up so we can start preparing lunch."

With Dinora out of the way, we could hopefully try to get to the bottom of this mess.

"Listen, here are the rules. You will speak one at a time. You'll both have the same amount of time to speak and no one will call the other out of their name. Got it?"

"Yes, Ms. Adams." They both responded simultaneously.

"Cherokee, you go first." I nodded over to her. Ninette folded her arms, pouting like a bratty five year old. I pointed at her. "Don't even start."

Cherokee went on and on about Ninette coming out of her room half dressed every time her boyfriend came over to visit her. Then Ninette went on about how Cherokee was just jealous of her because her boyfriend liked her and she knew he wanted to get with her. Ninette was only four months pregnant and still possessed a very nice shape. She didn't mind flaunting it. My mind couldn't stay focused on this nonsense between the two. I wanted to slap some sense into them both, but I listened to this mess for about thirty minutes.

After they finished spewing out this crap, I reeled them back in and reminded them both of the rules. "Ladies, the bottom line is this. We have rules in this home and one is we don't yell or scream at one another. Two, you respect the other members of the home. Ninette, we also have a dress code. I expect you to follow it if you don't want your privileges taken away. Do not come out of your room with just a towel wrapped around you. Cherokee, if she does break the rules, you're not to handle it yourself. You're to report it to the house manager or staff. Is that understood? Cherokee, you also need to think about what type of boyfriend you want and what type of boyfriend you have. If he's checking out your roommate right in your face while you're carrying his child, you might have a bigger problem than Ninette prancing around half naked."

The two ladies agreed to keep their cool and stay away from each other. I asked Ms. Wilma to write up the incident in the progress notes and an Incident form on each girl. I was ready to get out of there. As I rushed towards the door, Ms. Wilma ran after me and grabbed my hand, pulling me into the living room which was also our waiting/visiting area.

"Ms. Wilma, I know you want another weekend staff member and I'm trying but there's nothing I can do about that right now."

"I'm not worrying about that, right now. I have something else to tell you."

"What is it?"

"Last night I saw Angela outside talking to a man."

"And?"

"This man looked suspicious. He was really old. Not real old, but way too mature to be hanging around a sixteen year old. I asked her if he was her boyfriend. She said no. Then I asked her if it was her child's father. Again she said no."

"Well, what's the problem?"

"They weren't hugged up or anything like that, but he looked like he was up to something. They appeared very secretive. Something wasn't right. Whatever they were talking about upset her. She came in and went straight to her room. When I went in to question her about him, I could tell she'd been crying. Do you know where her father is? Or who he might be?"

"No, I don't. Just keep an eye on her. I'll try to talk to her later this week about it."

I drove up to my parent's house around three o'clock. When I reached the screen door, I could hear a lot of laughter coming from inside the house. I knocked on the weather-worn door while opening it to enter at the same time. "Hello!"

"We're in here, Brittney." Mom sounded surprisingly cheerful.

I strode through the formal living area to the step-down family room in the back of the house. My Aunt Libby, Mom and Dad were there watching old video tapes. Aunt Libby jumped up as soon as she saw me and grabbed me before I could prepare for the exorbitant hugs and kisses I received every time we were together.

"Hi, my Princess. How are you? You're just as beautiful as ever."

"Hi, Aunt Libby, I didn't know you were coming today. I'm so happy to see you." Aunt Libby nicknamed me Princess when I was a baby and most of the family called me Princess still. Aunt Libby was my father's sister and probably the only one in his racist family that truly loved me and my mom. I wondered if she knew about the pregnancy and the babies.

We laughed and talked all evening. My aunt seemed to bring out all that was good, kind, gentle and wonderful in Dad. My parents looked like a happily married couple. They looked like what I thought I remembered as a young child. I didn't always think Dad was mean and hateful. When did it all change?

"So, how long will you be here?"

"I'll be here for a few days. I'm going to Hawaii to meet up with some friends. I decided to make a stop here to see my favorite brother and sister-in-law."

"Who are you kidding? I'm your only brother." Dad nudged against her shoulder. They really had another brother but neither of them got along with him. Uncle Herbert, named after his father, disowned Dad and despised Libby for going against the family and supporting Dad and Mom's marriage.

"Yeah and I'm your only sister-in-law." Mom winked.

Aunt Libby laughed. "Well, you're still my favorites."

It was getting late. Mom and dad had had a few big yawns. I decided to call it a night, but not without trying to get Aunt Libby alone. I had to know if she knew anything about my brothers or how much of a tyrant her favorite brother really was.

"Why don't you come home with me so we can hang out?"

"I'd love to, sweetie, but I want to stay here with your mom and dad to catch up a little more. I promise my next trip you'll have me all to your pretty self. Okay?"

"That's fine." I kissed her good-bye and left disappointed I couldn't get any more information than I already had.

When I arrived home, I jumped on the computer again. There was so much information on missing people but all of the sites wanted you to pay. I Googled "how to find adopted siblings" but most of the sites that popped up weren't what I was looking for except one: Omnitrace. I filled out the online form with as many details as I'd gathered from Mom and prayed for the best. Mom said I was three years old when they were born, so they had to be thirty-two years old now. I read all of the testimonials on the site and imagined what it would be like meeting my brothers for the first time. Would we look alike? Would they resent me? What kind of teenage life did they have? Were they anything like Dad? Thoughts flooded my mind.

Also, I began to boil with rage, thinking of what Dad forced Mom to do. I couldn't conceive of a person using their own children as bargaining chips against one another. Well, being pissed off about it now wouldn't help me find them. I needed to focus only on finding my brothers for now.

Chapter Six

Libby grabbed Marilyn by the hand. "Come into my room so I can show you this new outfit I just bought." She closed the door behind them. "I want to know how you're really doing," Libby whispered.

"What are you talking about? I'm fine." Libby was the only family member that stood up to Richard when she heard him being cruel to Marilyn. She loved Marilyn like her own sister. There wasn't one other person in Richard's family that accepted Marilyn even after thirty-six years of marriage. He had two maternal aunts that blamed Marilyn for the death of their sister. His brother, Herbert Jr., despised her. His other sister, Nelda, wished she were dead. Libby knew Richard was no saint but he loved Marilyn and

Brittney more than anything. He just didn't know how to show it. He had too much of his father in him.

"I know Richard's not the easiest guy to live with. I know he's lost his temper with you on probably more than one occasion. I just want to know if you're okay."

Libby had expected her brother had been abusive but her suspicions were confirmed a few years ago when she dropped in unexpectedly for a visit.

****

Richard had stumbled in from his Friday night out with the boys. Marilyn rushed to serve his dinner to him. She sat the plate of baked chicken, peas and carrots and mashed potatoes in front of him. As she turned to get his glass of water and placed it perfectly at the side of his plate, he plopped down and looked at the meal in disgust before slapping it to the floor. "I'm a lieutenant, for God's sake! I don't have to eat chicken every day. What the hell is wrong with you? I'm sick of this." He jumped up and grabbed Marilyn by her arm. "Now get your lazy butt in the kitchen and fix me a decent meal."

"Please calm down, Richard. I'll cook something else. Just calm down." Marilyn pleaded. She immediately turned around and started searching through the refrigerator when she felt a violent shove in her back, thrusting her into the fridge. Richard snatched her by her hair and swung her around facing him, backhanding her across the face. She stumbled to the floor, hard. He picked her up by her clothes and pushed her back against the counter.

"Forget dinner. I think I'm ready for dessert." He kissed her swollen cheek.

The doorbell rang. "I have to get the door." Marilyn couldn't imagine who could be coming to the house at that hour but didn't care.

"No you don't. Whoever it is, they'll go away. You're not going anywhere." He clenched his fist towards her face, then slung her frail body towards the stove. He went towards her. She screamed, closing her eyes, waiting to feel that well-known sting from his rough hands. He laughed. Marilyn opened her eyes. As soon as she did, Richard delivered a strong slap across her face. His menacing eyes revealed he wanted her to see it coming. She screamed again, falling to the floor when she noticed an image in the window. Seconds later, she heard Libby's voice yelling and pounding on the front door.

"Let me in, Richard. Open this door now!"

Richard staggered to the door. Marilyn heard it open and him say, "Hey, how's my little sis?"

Libby pushed him away and ran into the kitchen. Marilyn was searching through the cabinets, trying to find something else to cook. "Marilyn? Are you all right?" Libby turned her around to examine her. A red welt covered the side of her face. Libby hugged her. Richard walked in. "She's fine. She's fixing supper right now, so leave her be."

"You big bully. I saw what happened. I stood right outside that window. I saw what you did to her."

"Listen here. What happens between me and my wife is none of your business."

"Well, I'm making it my business tonight. You need to go to your room and sleep it off, buddy." Libby puffed out her chest, soliciting a fight.

That was at least five years ago, but Libby always let Marilyn know she didn't forget and she was welcome in her home if she need a place of refuge.

****

"Libby, I'm fine. Let's just enjoy your visit and not worry about anything else. Your brother and I are doing well. It's your niece you should be concerned with. She doesn't give him a break, ever."

"Good for her. He probably doesn't deserve a break. Do you need me to talk to him while I'm here? You know he owes me big time."

"No. He's mellowed out a lot. What does he owe you big time for?"

"You know I was the only one in the family that supported him when he was dating you and when you two decided to get married." Libby laughed. "I'm not going to ever let him forget it. You know sometimes I need favors." Libby burst into deep laughter again.

"Well, I guess I owe you, too, huh."

"Sweetie, I believe you've paid all debts in full." Libby took Marilyn's hand with teary eyes. "Look, I know you love Richard, but you don't owe him your life. I want you to promise me if things get bad you'll call me. You're always welcome to stay with me."

"Right. That'll make Herbert Jr. and Nelda happy to see their black sister-in-law move in with you. They'd probably try to skin you alive." They both laughed. Then Marilyn's laugh turned quickly to tears and she hugged her tight. "I know I can always count on you."

"That's right." Seconds later, Libby jumped up. "Now let me show you the brochures for this lovely vacation I'm going on."

"Libby, I told Brittney about Jaden and Jerome."

Libby flopped back down, looking at Marilyn like she'd just seen a ghost. "Why on earth would you do that? Why would you want to live through that horrible time again?"

"I don't know. She caught me looking at the photos one evening. Then Richard came in and I told her to be quiet so she couldn't question me. She came back the next day and I could see it in her eyes she wasn't going to let up until she got some answers. I didn't have the energy to fight with her so I told her about them."

"Did you tell her everything?"

"Pretty much."

"I mean why you allowed Richard to have them taken away?"

"Yes, Libby. I had to. I had to let her know I wouldn't just give my own flesh and blood away for no good reason."

"Well, no wonder she hates her father."

"She hated him before then." Marilyn shrugged her shoulders.

Libby looked at her with one raised brow. "Now she hates and despises him even more. Which, I guess, I can't blame her." Libby snapped back from her temporary trance and stared at Marilyn. "How are you handling this? Are you going to tell Richard?"

"Have you lost your mind? He doesn't even know I stayed in contact with them...well not them but their whereabouts."

Libby shook her head. "I don't know. Sometimes it's better to just let sleeping dogs lie. How did Brittney react to all of this?"

"She wants to find them."

"Oh my God, girl. What have you done? What would be the point of that now? I need to talk some sense into Brittney."

"Before I knew what Richard had told the adoption agency, and God only knows who else, I imagined my boys would come searching for me, to find their real mother." Marilyn gave a sarcastic laugh. "Then I found out he told them I died in childbirth. The sickest thing about all this is I know Richard loves me. He gave up his entire family for me. He almost died just to be with me. I know he has some anger issues, hell he has a lot of issues, but I can't walk away. I can't leave him. He did the unspeakable, tearing my children away from me as soon as they came out of me. I swore I'd never forgive him but I did." Marilyn turned and looked at Libby. "Your racist family and the other entire dirty white South did a number on him. They ruined part of him. They brainwashed him. They ingrained a certain hatred in him. I believe that was the only reason he agreed with your father. He convinced him black men are no good and trouble. That they're hopeless, feeble minded and a danger to society. Your family had a Jim Crowism way of thinking and they embedded that way of thinking into Richard, especially about black men."

"Marilyn, what are you saying? Remember I'm Richard's family, too, and I'm not like that."

"You have to admit most of your family did and still does think like that. We're in the twenty first century and have a black president, and some of your family still hates me, simply because I'm black."

Libby looked as if she feared asking this question but had to. "Marilyn, do you love me? I mean like your family?"

"Of course I do. But you see, black people never had a problem with loving white people, at least most of us didn't. Libby, a lot of Richard's ways come from who he was raised by, and although I don't think he's racist, he does have a fear of black men. I know I shouldn't say this, but he doesn't want them to be over him at work, he doesn't want them to have more than he has and he definitely doesn't want one to marry his little Princess. He won't admit this to others or himself but I see it."

Chapter Seven

Peoplefinders.com sounded like they could help. I just needed to find a private investigator. I finally found one, Edward Benson, a former federal agent. I'd call him in the morning.

"Hello, everyone, how's everything this morning?" I cut my eyes over at Ninette and Cherokee as they were fixing their lunches for school. All the girls in the home had to be enrolled in an adult school if they didn't have a high school diploma or work if they did.

"It's a quiet morning and we're planning on keeping it that way, right?" Mary glared at Ninette and Cherokee.

Everyone left the house without a sound. I sat down and called Edward Benson to get some information on the cost and process for finding my brothers.

"Hello. May I speak with Edward Benson please?"

"This is Mr. Benson, how can I help you?"

"Hi. My name is Brittney Adams and I'd like some information on finding my brothers given up at birth, thirty-two years ago." Mr. Benson explained his process and his costs. I agreed to meet him in his office tomorrow at noon. I was so excited but needed to give him as much information as possible to expedite the process. I needed to reach Mom today. I needed pictures and the exact names of the adoption agency and foster homes and any other information she might have forgotten to give to me.

I arrived at Mom's house around four o'clock. Mom and Aunt Libby were in the kitchen cooking. I didn't see Dad's car nor did I expect to see it. He usually got home around six most evenings. I wasn't sure if Aunt Libby knew about my brothers so I decided not to mention anything about Jerome and Jaden until I could get my mother alone. I stood at the kitchen door unnoticed, watching Aunt Libby and Mom standing side by side at the counter next to the sink cutting vegetables. The two ladies were so close – like blood sisters. Aunt Libby was my protector at Dad's family gatherings, the few times I attended them.

Aunt Libby said, "I still think I should talk some sense into Princess. I see no need to stir up the past."

"Hello, ladies." They both turned and looked at me as if I were an intruder. "I planned on waiting to discuss my brothers with you, but I see there's no need for that."

"Princess, I know you're all gung ho about finding your brothers. You need to think about the impact this will have on your mother, your brothers and their families and your father." Aunt Libby said.

"I know you don't really believe I give a rat's butt about my father's feelings in all this."

"Look, you two, let's just settle down and discuss this calmly." Mom walked to the table and gestured for Aunt Libby and me to join her.

"Mom, I need as much information as you can provide. I have an appointment with a private investigator tomorrow and I want to give him everything we know about Jerome and Jaden. Aunt Libby, if you have any information, I'd appreciate it if you'd give that to me as well."

"Have you thought about this? Do you understand that maybe these boys...or rather men, might not want to have you rambling through their lives, bringing up their past. Maybe they're happy with their families. Maybe Jaden doesn't even know he was adopted. Have you thought about that, young lady? You're being very selfish right now." Aunt Libby scolded me, but I didn't care.

"If you don't want to help me, that's fine." I leaned towards my mother. "Mom, you owe this to yourself, me and my brothers. They have a right to know who their blood is. They have a right to know their real mother and...their sister. Please, Mom, I need the pictures and any other information you remember so I can give it to the private investigator."

"I don't know why I told you about them."

"I think you told me because you want to see them. You want them to know you before you leave this earth. You knew I wouldn't keep this information without acting on it. You know me too well for that."

"Oh my God, Marilyn. Princess is telling the truth, isn't she? We all know how headstrong she is. You knew that come hell or high water, Princess would find them. What I don't understand is how were you planning on handling Richard through all of this?"

"Maybe she made up her mind about Dad, too. Are you planning on leaving him finally?"

"No, I'm not planning on leaving your father." Mom paused. "I guess I didn't consider the ramifications of my confession. Princess, I agree with Libby. I'm sorry for burdening you with this, but I think it'd be best for everyone if we let this go before anyone gets hurt. The past should be left in the past. We shouldn't disrupt your brothers' lives just because I was feeling guilty and longing for my sons." Mom heaved a sigh of relief. "Please, let this go, for me."

"Sorry. I can't do that." I ran into the bedroom and began searching for the shoebox. I found it, just where I'd last seen it. I quickly ripped it open and collected the two photos and paperwork she had on one of the foster families where Jerome had lived as a child. I replaced the shoebox under the blankets. As I turned to leave, Aunt Libby and Mom stood blocking the door.

"Princess, I'm asking you to leave this alone. Do this for me. I can't relive the pain of my past. I just can't." Mom began to weep but surprisingly, I had no sympathy for her. I quickly bolted my way past Mom and Aunt Libby and left, determined to find my brothers.

The next day I decided not to go to Ebony Eyes. Instead, I copied the photos and typed up the information I had on Jerome and Jaden to present to the private investigator. My cell phone rang. I checked the caller ID. It was Matthew. "Hello."

"Hello, Ms. Brittney. How are you this morning?"

"Great. How are you?"

"I'd be great, too, if you agree to have lunch with me today."

"I'm sorry. I have an appointment at noon. Can I take a rain check?"

"Would I sound too desperate to ask if I could have dinner with you?"

"Not at all. I'd love to have dinner with you tonight. How does seven thirty sound?"

"Good. I'll see you then."

"Okay, bye."

I arrived at the Daily Grill on Ventura Blvd. ten minutes before noon. I asked to be seated at a table near the front and notified the waitress I expected a Mr. Edward Benson. Not five minutes after I arrived, a tall, neatly trimmed middle-aged man walked in and said, "I'm expecting a Ms. Brittney…"

I waved my hand. "I'm here." I sprung from the chair and rushed over to greet him. We sat reviewing the process for finding Jerome and Jaden and costs again. Mr. Benson explained the stats for finding children that had been adopted. He proudly boasted that although the stats aren't great, he usually had a ninety-five percent recovery rate. He was absolutely sure I had enough information to find Jerome and Jaden. I was so excited I barely ate the Fish and Chips platter I had ordered.

When I arrived at Ebony Eyes, I noticed the newest resident, Angela, walking around to the back of the house. It was too early for her to already be out of school. I parked my car across the street a couple of doors down. I tiptoed around the side of the house and peeked in the back. Angela was talking on her cell to someone.

"I already told you I don't know what I'm going to do. Why can't you leave me alone? I'm at home but I don't want you coming over here again. Just leave me alone!" She slammed the flip phone shut and buried her head in her hands crying. I decided not to question her now but to keep a close watch on her. She was new to our home and obviously more troubled than I'd thought. I needed to win her trust first. I tiptoed back to the front of the house, unlocked the door and went in. About thirty minutes later Angela rang the doorbell. We didn't allow any of the girls to have keys to the house because this was a twenty-four hour facility. Therefore, staff had to be there any time a resident was there.

"Hi, Angela. You're here early today. Did class let out early?"

She snapped defensively, "No. I didn't feel good, that's all."

"Well, you know the rules. If you need to come home early, you need to have someone call me or Ms. Cooper so we can meet you here to let you in." Angela stood quietly listening. This sixteen-year-old girl looked as if she had the weight of the world on her shoulders. Her face was long, her eyes drained and her body beaten with stress. No sixteen year old should look like this. "Are you feeling okay now?"

"Yes. I feel better."

"Do you want something to eat?"

"No. I just wanna lay down."

"Good. I'll come up and check on you later. You know, Angela, if you need to talk about anything, I'm here. If you don't want to talk to me, you can always talk to a therapist. We're not here just to house you until your baby is born. We're here to help you grow mentally, emotionally and physically. I know it's hard to be in a new place at this critical time in your life."

She struggled to detain the tears from overflowing. "Could I go lay down now?"

"Sure, sweetie. I'll come up later to check on you."

Forty-five minutes later Ms. Gayle Wright, another staffer, came in. Ms. Cooper was running late. The other three girls trickled in about ten minutes later. I stayed until Ms. Cooper arrived. I wanted to personally notify her about Angela's behavior so she could keep an eye on her.

I arrived home shortly after six. Although I felt an enormous amount of stress, between trying to find my brothers and what was going on with Angela, I was excited about seeing Matthew again. I hadn't been in, or even thought of being in, a relationship for such a long time. I felt nervous but comfortable with Matthew. For some reason I felt I could trust him. He didn't seem like the type to play games. Matthew almost seemed too good to be true. No children, no ex-wives and no psychiatric issues from a dreadful childhood.

I slipped into a fitted orange dress that hugged every curve perfectly. A long slit ran up the side of my long toned legs. The back was cut so low it barely left room for the imagination, but it did. With my four and a half inch stilettos, I stood just under six feet.

The doorbell rang. I hoped he'd like the dress. I didn't want to look too sleazy. I didn't want to give him the wrong impression. Oh, but I did wanna look sexy. "Coming."

When I opened the door, Matthew stepped in, immediately hugged me and kissed me on my cheek. He smelled so good. I didn't know what type of cologne he wore, but it made me want to jump on him and wrap my long legs around him for the night. "Well hello to you, too."

"Hello, Ms. Brittney." I took him by his hand and escorted him to the couch in the living room.

"So what are the plans for tonight? Do we need to rush out? Or do we have time to sit and chat for a while?"

"Since it's a weeknight, I didn't think it was necessary to make reservations so we can chat if you're not hungry now."

"How has your week been so far?"

Before he answered, he glared at me. "That dress is hot." He gave a devilish smile. "My week has been fine so far. What about yours?"

"Busy but very productive."

"Do you have some big event coming up?"

"As a matter of fact, I do. This Saturday is the Women's Networking High Tea and Fashion Show event I've been working on for the past few months. You just made me remember, I need to get in touch with my promotions guy I hired. I have to follow-up with the newspaper editors I submitted articles to as well." The past couple of days, I had become so involved with looking for my brothers, I'd left some loose ends for my client's networking event.

"Wow, doesn't seem like you have too much time for me tonight."

I laughed because I did recall a lot of things I still had to do this week. "I think I can muster up a little time for you."

"We better get started before you start thinking of other tasks you've forgotten."

On the way to the restaurant, Matthew shared general information about some of his parolees, discreetly leaving out names, and I told him about my residents, specifically Angela. I expressed my concern for her. There was something different about her. He offered to check the mysterious guy out if we found out his name, to see if he had any kind of criminal background so we would at least know what we were dealing with.

By the time we arrived at the restaurant, I was sure Matthew could probably help me find Jerome and Jaden. He had more access to personal information than I imagined. I'd already given Mr. Benson a deposit. Besides, he wasn't very expensive. Free was always better.

We were promptly seated; The atmosphere was elegant and romantic. I ordered the Pistachio Crusted Salmon and Matthew ordered the New York Steak. We both seemed comfortable with each other and talked as if we'd known each other for years.

"Well, I know you have a lot on your plate so I won't keep you out too long. I have a new parolee coming in the morning also. This guy has a long C-file. The whole so-called rehabilitation program really doesn't work for these repeat offenders. I hope this one has learned something during his incarceration for the past ten years."

"Do you ever get scared working with all of those crim-inals? I know you're big and muscular." I laughed. "You look like you can take on a few linebackers by yourself, but still, these are guys with horrific crimes."

"No. I guess they don't scare me because I grew up in the hood. I grew up with some of the most dangerous thugs around. They didn't scare me then and they definitely don't scare me now."

"Spoken like a true macho man." I tilted my glass of wine to him.

We returned to my house just before ten o'clock. I in-vited Matthew in for coffee. He declined the coffee but stayed for my lemon pudding pound cake. A couple of hours had flown by when he decided to leave. I walked him to the door and was pleasantly surprised when he pulled me close and kissed me over and over again. I didn't want this night to end, but I didn't want him to think I went around giving up the goods just because a gorgeous man treated me to a nice dinner and good conversation. I peeled myself from him. "Good-bye."

Ms. Cooper called me at eight o'clock the next morning to notify me Angela said she felt ill and didn't want to go to school this morning. She asked if I could come over to stay with her while she ran her errands. I showered, gathered my briefcase and was at Ebony Eyes within forty minutes. Sandra and Cherokee were just grabbing their lunches as I entered the kitchen. Ms. Cooper walked Ninette, Cherokee, Maria and Sandra to the door to make sure they were completely out of the house. She rushed to my office to tell me the night staff reported last night Angela screamed in terror several times. She kept saying, "No! Don't! Please don't do this!" When the staff woke her up from the nightmare, they tried to get her to tell them what had her so frightened. She just cried and wouldn't speak.

There was something going on. This was not just the run of the mill teenage pregnancy. Where was the company she was so anxious to receive when she moved in? No one stopped by to visit her except that older man who was seen sneaking around. It didn't appear to be an enjoyable visit from what Ms. Cooper had caught a glimpse of.

Angela was still in bed. I went upstairs to her room to speak with her. I knocked on the door, but she didn't answer. I knocked again this time, harder. Still no answer. I opened the door and walked in. She had her body turned towards the wall, away from the door. I lightly shook her. "Angela, wake up." She moaned and moved away from me. "Angela. You need to wake up."

"What? I told Ms Cooper I wasn't feeling good."

"I understand, but I need to know what's bothering you. Do I need to take you to see a doctor or...?"

"No. I just need to rest, I have a headache and I'm a little nauseous. That's all."

"All right. I'll be downstairs if you need anything." I left Angela's room determined to find out what was going on with her. I went to my office downstairs and searched through Angela's file to find her mother's phone number. I decided to wait before I worried her mother about this, so I wrote the number down on a piece of paper and placed it in my purse.

I called the newspaper editor of the *L.A. Times*, the *Daily News*, and *L.A. Weekly*. I called the caterers and the decorators to make sure everyone was on-point for the event. I reviewed every detail. Before I knew it, it was eleven forty-five and my stomach growled, reminding me I hadn't eaten all day.

Angela peeked around the corner. "Good morning."

"Hey. Come on in. Are you feeling better?"

"Yes, but I'm starving."

"Me, too. Do you feel like taking a ride with me to get some junk food?"

Her eyes lit up. "Yes. What kinda junk food?"

"Anything you want. As long as it's not too far. Hurry up and get dressed."

Angela split out of the office and was back down dressed, within minutes.

She chose to go to In-N-Out, which was fine with me. I loved their fries. Since the home is just blocks from Sunset, it was a straight shot. It wouldn't take too long to get there. Although there were a lot of other fast-food places closer, like I said, I loved their fries. She ordered a double-double meal and I ordered the same, only protein style for me. I was already pushing it with the fries. I wasn't about to add the bread as well. We opted to sit outside. It was a beautiful day. This was the first time I'd seen Angela looking like a sixteen year old. I felt this was a good time to ask her some personal questions.

"Angela, do you speak to the father of your child?"

She snapped. "No. My baby don't have a father."

"Every child has a father. It might not be one we're proud to call the father, but they're still the father just the same. I take it you two broke up?"

"How can you break up with someone you were never with?"

"What are you saying? This was a one time thing?"

She stopped eating and stared out towards the busy street. "Something like that. Can we drop the subject?"

"Sure."

Living with my parents, I knew the signs of abuse. I was positive Angela had experienced some form of abuse, but I wasn't sure of what kind, or from whom. Her mother didn't seem like the abusive type, but she definitely didn't express much concern for her sixteen-year-old daughter, either. I tried to keep communications open by asking about school and her goals. "So, Angela, what college do you want to attend when you finish school?" She looked surprised.

"I didn't think I could still go to college. Mom said all that was over now."

"It doesn't have to be. That's up to you. It won't be easy, but you can still go to college. What do you want to be?"

A dismal expression came over her. "I don't know."

"Well you should start thinking about it."

We finished our meals. I didn't get the information I wanted, but this was a start.

When we arrived back at the home, I received a call from Mr. Benson. He'd already obtained information on Jerome. He was living in Prince George's County in Maryland. He worked as a lawyer at Tate, Tate and Brown Law Firm. Mr. Benson gave me the phone number to the law firm. Just hearing this news, my palms became sweaty and chills covered my body. I could feel the pounding of my heart trying to escape my chest. As Mr. Benson was still talking, my mind wandered, *how would Jerome take this news? How and when should I contact him? Would he shut the door in my face or hang up on me?*

"Ms. Adams? Are you still there?"

"Oh, yes, I'm sorry. You said he was a lawyer and worked and lived in Prince George's County. Do you have any other information on him?"

"Yes. There appears to be no wife or children. As a matter of fact, there doesn't seem to be any other living family member. Mother deceased, father unknown, and no siblings. As you said, he moved from foster family to foster family. However, he received a couple of Academic Scholarships. He attended the University of Chicago where he graduated with his Law degree. A very smart young man."

For the first time since I found out about my brothers, I seriously considered not contacting him. It seemed he had a wonderful life. Why induct him into this dysfunctional life Mom and Dad called home? After all he had endured, being tossed from home to home as a child. Why mess his life up now?

"Ms. Adams?"

"Yes. Is there anything else?"

"Yes. I don't have much on Jaden yet, but he has been incarcerated on several different occasions for petty theft. I should have more information by the end of this week at the latest."

"Okay, thank you for getting this information to me so quickly. I'll talk to you later."

"Remember, my recommendation is that I contact your siblings first. Let me know when you're ready."

"Ok. Will do."

"Have a good evening, Ms. Adams."

"You too, Mr. Benson."

What do I do now? The thought of picking up the phone and contacting my brother I never knew existed before a few days ago was now a reality. Was I being selfish? No, I wasn't being selfish. I had a right to know my blood brother. Although it seemed he had a wonderful life, he might have longed to have his own family. Besides, there was nothing wrong with me. It was Mom and Dad that were in a dysfunctional relationship. I went home and sat for hours contemplating what to do.

Chapter Eight

"Mr. Roclin, your client Mr. Temple is here to see you."

"Send him in."

Jerome cleared the files from his desk and closed his briefcase. His desk was unusually placed catty-cornered so he could see his front door and have a great view from the wall to wall window at the north side of his office that overlooked a lavishly landscaped courtyard which featured a huge waterfall. His office walls showcased a host of plaques and certificates he'd received over the years. His accomplishments had succeeded many for his young age. His décor was impeccable. From the Mocha Cherry stylish desk to the huge wall to wall book cabinet that seemed to house hundreds of law journals. The office was the size of a small conference room.

Mr. Temple knocked and peeked in the half cracked door. "Come on in, Allen. How are you?"

"As well as expected, I guess." Mr. Temple shook hands with Jerome, seemingly a bit nervous, but appeared ready to go over his consultation with him.

"Well let's go over the case. How's your son holding up?"

"Ryan is fine, but I think my wife is going to go crazy if we don't hurry up and get him out of jail."

"He's going to be arraigned this afternoon. He's never had a run-in with the law so it shouldn't be a problem to get him out on bail." Jerome leaned back in his oversized chocolate leather chair. "The only problem..." he noticed Mr. Temple's eyes shift up, "or rather issue with this case is the woman identified Ryan as her attacker. She claims he ran away before an actual rape – which is good. On the other hand, there's no semen, so we can't use DNA to prove his innocence. I have a little work cut out for me, but I'm still positive we'll have a good outcome. She's a little flaky on part of her story so I'm sure I can break her down. I just don't want to have to do it in court. Jurors tend to, of course, be more sympathetic towards victims."

Jerome Roclin had been practicing law for the past seven years. He'd grown quite a reputation in the community for successfully defending young black men in cases against them. He realized at a young age there was little to no help for people who looked like him. His entire life was a struggle and there was no one he could turn to that would speak up for him – at least no one he knew of. Although he defended the poor, he was paid very well by Tate, Tate, and Brown. The law firm had a department dedicated to representing minorities and lower income citizens. Jerome also was allowed to take six pro bono cases per year. He was very selective.

"Can I ask you a question?" Mr. Temple leaned in and scratched his head. Mr. Temple was small in stature. He was bald at the top with a short afro surrounding the perimeter of his head.

"Sure. What's up?"

"You work in this huge law firm. This firm makes a lot of money and by the looks of this office and your clothes, so do you. I did some research of my own and I know this company is doing very well because it takes on commercial cases with big organizations. I mean you guys do it all. So why do you also defend the lower class? Or lower income, I should say. It's not like you all need our little pennies."

Jerome laughed. "Well, Mr. Temple, we also believe in taking care of our community and giving back every chance we get. Actually, that's what attracted me to this firm. Coming from very humble beginnings, myself, I believe in helping the less fortunate."

"You come from humble beginnings, you say? I see you as one of those kids that had well-to-do parents that pushed you to exceed in everything and wouldn't allow you to be anything less than a doctor or lawyer." Mr. Temple chuckled raised an eyebrow and nodded in agreement with himself.

Jerome waved his index finger back and forth at Mr. Temple. "No, sir, I didn't have any part in that fairy tale. My mother died when I was born, and my father didn't want me. That's all I know. He could be dead, too. Who knows? I grew up in the foster care system. I bounced from place to place until I was fifteen. I remained in that particular home where I was ridiculed and told I was nothing and never would be anything everyday until I graduated from high school and went off to college. Allow me to give you a quick synopsis of my life. As I stated, I lived in numerous foster homes growing up and each time I entered a new home, I entered a different kind of abuse, a different kind of personal hell I had to endure. I was an angry boy. I learned at an early age not to trust adults or anybody else. I hated living and I remember many times wishing I was dead. I'm not sure what it was that kept me from killing myself, although, I did try but that's another story. I know now it was by the grace of God that kept me here. One home I was in I remember vividly the man, Mr. Landers, used to beat me for his personal recreation. I was sent home early from school one day because I was sick. The school nurse said I had a fever and she had to call my foster parents. We lived down the street from the school so they allowed me to walk home. When I walked in that house Mr. Landers gave me the coldest evil stare. His bloodshot red eyes tore through me and I knew I probably wouldn't survive the beating I was about to get. By this time I didn't care. I shot that cold stare right back at him. Mr. Landers was disappointed he didn't see that frightened little boy." Jerome chuckled. "They say the eyes are the entrance to your soul. Well, I guess my soul, my spirit had accepted death. I stood there as tall as a helpless nine-year-old boy could stand ready to die. I think I even egged him on by shooting daggers with my eyes. I said, 'The nurse said I should have some juice and go straight to bed.'

"Mr. Landers hovered over me like a giant Joe cool puffing on a cigarette. He took the cigarette out of his mouth and blew the smoke right down on me, and said, 'Is that right?'

"I stuck out my tiny bird chest and said, 'Yeah, that's right.' I guess I really wanted to die that day. In a split second, I felt a hot sting across my face and was lying on the floor, but I wasn't crying. Instead I lifted my head up towards Mr. Landers and said, 'Is that all you got?' Yeah, I definitely wanted to die that day. That man started pounding on me and yelling, 'You little bastard, who do you think you are talking to like that? Don't you know I will kill you?' He picked me up by my neck. His big hands were wrapped around my neck. I could taste the blood from my busted lips. He threw me down to the floor and began stomping and kicking me. I moaned from the excruciating pain that pierced through my body. I thought this would never end and then I felt a blow to my head and that was it. It was over. I woke up a few hours later in the hospital. That was just one of my wonderful childhood memories. Doesn't sound like the dream childhood you pictured, huh?"

Mr. Temple said, "Man, I'm sorry. I'm apologizing to you for that idiot that did that to you and for all the other men who hurt you."

"It's okay. As you can see, I survived. God wrapped his arms around me; protecting me from death. He also sent me my personal guardian angel, Mr. Williams. When I was in the hospital, I met a man that became my mentor. From that time I spent in the hospital, he watched over me. He was doing volunteer work there. He gave me his number and told me I could call him anytime. I called him about a month later and we stayed in touch. He was very instrumental in helping me slay the demons trying to possess me. I focused on school and ended up graduating with honors and obtaining a fully paid academic scholarship to a four year college. All because one man took the time to care for and mentor me. Something so simple made the difference in me growing up to be someone who may rob you to someone who can help you and others. To make a long story short, that's why I do what I do to help our youth."

When Jerome finished his story, Mr. Temple's eyes became misty. "I'm glad you accepted our case. Thank you so much." He extended his hand to shake Jerome's hand.

"Good, enough chit chat. Let's see about getting your son out of this mess."

Chapter Nine

"Ms. Cooper, I hope you have extra staff at your beck and call for the next two days because I'll be unavailable. Remember the Women's High Tea is this weekend and we're expecting over three hundred women. I'll be working like a modern day slave for the next couple of days."

"Yes, I remember. Don't worry about the girls. We have everything under control for the moment."

After speaking with Ms. Cooper, I began dialing the few assistants I had for this event to confirm our meeting for this afternoon hoping everyone would keep their egos in check. Working with women, some women, could be very difficult. I called all six ladies, getting each to confirm they'd be on time and ready to work at Karen's house by noon. I'm glad there was no time for me to think about Jerome. I'd make a decision after this weekend.

I stopped by Mom's house to check in. I loved it when my aunt Libby was visiting. There was an air of peacefulness; although, my last visit was a bit contentious. I decided I wouldn't tell them I had information on Jerome's whereabouts until I knew for sure what I was going to do.

The door was unlocked so I walked in. There was no one in the living room. I headed for the kitchen where I saw Mom standing over the kitchen sink looking out the window appearing to be deep in thought. I watched her for a few seconds before making myself known. "Hey, Mom, how's it going?"

Mom grabbed me, hugging me tight as usual. "Hey, Princess, how's my beautiful daughter?"

"I'm great. Just busy. Are you and Aunt Libby coming to the High Tea and Fashion Show this Saturday?"

"That's this Saturday? Oh no, we'll have to miss it. Libby and I are going with your father to the Annual Police Fundraiser that day."

"That's not until late evening. The Fashion Show is at noon. You can do both."

Aunt Libby walked in yelling, "I want to go to the Fashion Show, too! Hey, Princess." She wrapped her massive chalky white hands around my face, planting a big, sloppy wet kiss on my forehead. "Now what's going on in here? What fashion show am I claiming to want to go to?"

"Well, I have a big event planned for this Saturday. It's for WNG, Women Networking Group. Remember my friend Adrienne Hampton from school? She's the founder of WNG. Her company does business consulting for small business owners. Every year she has an event to showcase the top five small businesses and features them at the event. She has a different theme every year. This year's theme is fashion. One of the women featured is a new designer, Tamila Preston. Adrienne thought this event would also be a way to launch some of Tamila's new fall designs. You two have to come. I know it's the same day as the department's fundraiser, but you will be back in time to rest before going out that evening." By now I'd slipped into little girl status, begging and whining for them to attend.

"Besides, this is for Adrienne." I looked at Mom.

"You know she'd be ecstatic to see you again." Adrienne and I grew up together. She was the only person I trusted and confided in at school.

"I'll check with your father to see if he minds."

Aunt Libby and I both turned and looked at Mom in astonishment. Before I could speak, Aunt Libby said, "Why do you need to check with Richard? He's not your daddy. You do not need his permission to attend your daughter's event. Remember, she's the planner. This is very important to her. You should be there to support her."

"Libby, when you're married, you discuss your plans with your spouse out of respect for each other and your marriage." Mom seemed to need to justify her comment.

"I understand that." Aunt Libby folded her arms and shifted her weight to her side. "Does Richard discuss his plans with you, too, or does he just tell you he's going to such and such place with an attitude that dares you to question him? I'm all for that respect thing, but it has to be the same rules for both parties."

Whoever started the myth white women are more submissive didn't know my Aunt Libby. Or maybe she has a little black in her blood because she's one feisty woman. I could tell she hurt Mom's feelings, but the truth hurt.

Mom turned to me., "Like I said, I'll check with your father. Now I'd rather discuss something else. Have you checked into finding your brothers?" Again she shocked Aunt Libby and me with this question. Aunt Libby glared at me and shrugged her shoulders.

"Why? I thought you wanted me to leave that alone."

"Yes. I'm just making sure you're leaving the whole situation alone."

"Mom, I've been so busy lately, I haven't had a lot of time to think about it." I could tell the way she looked at me she knew I was lying. "I would like to know more information about them. I know you said you felt you had to do this, give them away, but I still don't understand why you didn't try to find them after I'd grown up. Weren't you the least bit curious to know how your sons were doing? If you had grandchildren?"

"You're determined to make me miserable, aren't you? Of course I've wondered about my sons. There's not a day that goes by I don't think about them. I don't have the right to interfere in their lives after giving them away like that. I have no right." She yelled. "I want to know is there any way you could find them just to see if they're okay? To maybe get an updated picture of them and their families if they have wives and children. I'd like that. Your father would never have to know."

I was good until she mentioned Dad not having to know. Then I blew up. "Why in the world are you still so concerned about what he thinks? Who cares about him knowing? He needs to face this horrendous thing he did, anyway. He had no right to do this! Why do you feel you owe him your life? Is it because he almost lost his when he was dating you? Mom, you don't owe him anything. You both sacrificed a great deal to be together, not just him. Those sick white racists caused problems for you and your family, too." I looked at Aunt Libby. "No offense."

"None taken, sweetie. I know first-hand how sick they were and still are. I can tell you some stories that would blow your mind, little girl."

Whenever Aunt Libby called me "little girl," she was telling me "you don't know as much as you think you know" and was usually about to school me.

Mom reached out and took my hand and gazed straight into my eyes. "Brittney, I still have my family. My family never turned their back on me but your father, besides from Libby, lost his entire family. He chose me over his family."

"Now wait a minute, Marilyn. I'm with Britt on this one. You don't owe him your life because of things that happened in the past. Like I said before, Richard is my brother. I love him to pieces, but I love you, too. I've seen you go from a bold, beautiful, highly intelligent, spirit-filled, motivated woman to a timid, fearful, reticent, intimidated little girl. I don't mean to be harsh, but you need to find your spine again."

Mom looked confused. As much as I agreed with Aunt Libby, I didn't want to make Mom's life any worse than I believed it already was. I thought she had convinced herself her life wasn't that bad. I threw my hands up. "I can't do this today. We'll get together and talk about this later." I kissed them each on their cheek and walked out before anyone else could say anything that might draw me back into the conversation.

As I drove home, I thought maybe there was a lot I didn't understand. When you take those vows for better or for worse, it didn't give a timeline on the worse. What if your whole marriage was the worse? Maybe that was what Mom was doing, sticking by her man through the worse. I'm not a big fan of the church, but I don't think God intended for women to live the rest of their lives in misery because they chose the wrong man. Oh well, if she thought she had a good marriage, who was I to tell her it wasn't? Dad would have to face his past sooner or later.

The 101 freeway wasn't bad; I made it home in twenty minutes. My home was nestled between my parent's home in Sherman Oaks and Ebony Eyes just outside of West Hollywood. I checked my voice mail and was surprised to hear a message from Adrienne. I wondered why she didn't call my cell. I wanted to tell her everything I recently learned, but this wasn't the time. She had enough on her plate right now. We both wanted this weekend to be a huge success. She'd attracted so much business through her annual events, and this one was going to be the largest yet. Because of the massive turnout in the previous years, many vendors wanted to be a part of the event this year. We had to move the event to the largest banquet room at the hotel. This was also one of my biggest events I'd planned. I hit a gold mine with the two assistants I hired. They were highly self-motivated and very creative. I didn't know how I would have made it without them. I took off my clothes, slipped into one of my sleepshirts and climbed into my big La-Z-Boy before calling Adrienne. I knew this call would take a while so I wanted to get comfy.

"Hi Adrienne, it's me. I just got home and heard your message."

"Hey, Britt, are you as worn out and anxious as I am?"

"Of course I am. Everything is going to be perfect, so don't worry. When it's all over, we're going to take a well deserved trip to Burke Williams Spa, then to a nice restaurant and fill our tummies with some good food. We'll laugh and talk about how wonderful the event was. We'll probably laugh about the things that went wrong that no one else knew about."

"You always make me feel better. Thanks. I'm going to hold you to that Spa day."

"That won't be a problem. Now let's go through our updates."

"All right. I met with all of the featured business owners today. We have five, including Tamila. Her fall fashions are awesome. We're going to have to add shopping to our Spa day because girly is going to have to hook us both up."

"You know I'm down for some shopping." We both laughed. My professional side disappeared for a moment as we engaged in some small talk about our old wardrobes. "Tell me who the honored guests are again, what business they are each in, and in which order they'll be speaking. You know, the rundown of the program, but Britt style."

"Okay, Britt style, so you don't want a bunch of details, huh. Give it to you quick and easy to digest. Girl, you're a mess." Adrienne laughed. "Here goes. I'm doing intros and thanking everyone, blah, blah, blah. First up is Michelle Bowie, founder of Bowie's Cleaning Services. Next is Chrystal Knight, financial planner. This chick has it together. We're going to have to meet with her. I've spoken with a few of her clients. Next, we have Audrey Calhoun, director of her own travel business. And a special tribute to a young girl name Channel Brown who has started her own bakery. I really want to encourage her so I'll be presenting a special gift of encouragement to her at the end of the program. Lastly, Tamila Preston, fashion designer. She's blowing up already so it's good she's with us this year. The dress rehearsal is scheduled for tomorrow. That's the rundown. What do you think?"

"Sounds good. Do you think we're going to be able to stick to the timeline?"

"Yeah, without a problem." Adrienne said with a confidence that scared me. "But we do have the room until five thirty,. right?"

"Yes. I've notified all of the vendors to be there no later than ten. The committee and I will be there by nine."

We went over the plans in detail for hours before the hunger pangs started talking to me. I finally ended the call. I pulled out the old Foreman Grill and threw two small turkey patties on it. I cut onions, tomatoes, and lettuce, opened the lid when the patties were done and slid a slice of cheese on each patty. Ummmm, it was the best double cheeseburger made in history.

I took a quick shower and was climbing into bed when the phone rang. I was wiped out and in no mood to talk on the phone until I spotted the Caller ID. It was Matthew. I definitely had time to make small talk with him.

I quickly grabbed the phone. "Hello."

"Hello, Ms Brittney. This is Matthew."

"I know. How was your day?"

"Very busy. I'm sorry for calling you so late but I really wanted to hear your voice."

"It's okay. I was just getting into bed. Your call is a pleasant interruption of my beauty sleep." We both laughed.

"Well, how was your day? I know your event is in a couple of days, right?"

"Yes, and I've been working like a dog but everything is coming along just fine." We talked for about an hour before my yawns started coming more frequently. By then we both decided to hang up and finish our conversation later.

My stomach was in knots. I had never been so nervous at an event. I was usually the cool, calm, collected one while everyone around me freaked out.

That was my biggest event to date. Matthew showed up in a gorgeous Armani suit. He tended to be a little rough around the edges so I was surprised to see him so sophisticated and poised. My aunt Libby even got my mom to come out to support me. The speakers all presented their businesses well and the fashion show was a smash. Ebony Fashion Show didn't have anything on that. I was stunned to learn that the show was the first for most of the models.

I met at least ten potential clients from that event. Not that I needed any extra business right now, but I did enjoy planning. I spoke with most of the vendors and business was good for them as well. Half of them already told me they would definitely be back next year.

Aunt Libby and Mom told me they'd have to leave immediately after closing remarks so Dad wouldn't have a hissy fit. Well, they didn't tell me that, but I knew the reason why the sudden need to depart.

"Britt," Mom called out, waving to get my attention. I walked over to them. Matthew sat at the table with them. Although this wasn't planned, it was a nice setting for them to get to know each other.

"Hey. Did you have a good time?"

"It was really nice," they all chimed in together with huge smiles on their faces.

"You did an excellent job. I'm impressed." Matthew stared at me like he couldn't wait to get me home. If he only knew the only thing I planned tonight was to get under some covers, alone, with a cup of hot cocoa in one hand, the TV remote in the other.

"Thank you. Glad you enjoyed yourself."

"Well, Princess, we have to go now. I know you're tired, but your father would be very happy if you decided to join us tonight."

"I'm so tired I can barely see straight. I won't be able to join you guys tonight. You know how I feel about those functions anyway."

"We don't have to get ugly about it here." Mom cut her eyes toward Matthew. She believed in keeping dirty laundry well hidden.

I hugged and kissed Aunt Libby and Mom and said good-bye. Matthew and I watched them for a few seconds, making their way through the crowd of people that still lingered behind conversing and networking.

"I hope you're not too tired to have dinner with me tonight. Remember I told you I wanted to take you out to celebrate."

"I remember. I can't stay out too late. I really need to get some rest."

"Sounds good. Do you want me to help you clean things up or help with whatever? I see the hotel people are getting the tables. What exactly are you responsible for?"

"Not much at this point. I just need to talk to the coordinator and sign some paperwork. If you don't mind, we could go straight from here. You can follow me home. I'll take a quick shower. Then I'll be all yours." Matthew's eyebrows rose up. "For a couple of hours...to eat...food...Matthew." We giggled.

"Don't worry. I got it." Matthew had a devious smile.

After I signed the paperwork, Matthew and I walked to our cars. We were parked on the same row. Matthew walked me to my car. "I forgot I have a quick errand to run. I should be at your house by the time you finish showering."

"Okay." He gave me a peck on the cheek, opened my door, and waited until I was safely strapped in before walking away.

I was happy the event was held at the Sheraton Gateway hotel. I didn't have to drive too far to get home. I pulled into my garage just shy of thirty minutes later. I rushed to my room, jumped in the shower, and prayed Matthew would be there by the time I got out because if he wasn't, I would probably fall asleep waiting for him. As I rubbed lotion over my legs, I heard the doorbell. Thank God I didn't have to wait. I was so drained. I grabbed my wrap-around dress and tied it while trotting to the door. I opened the door and to my surprise, Matthew was standing there in some nice jeans and a shirt, holding bags of what smelled like Chinese food.

"What's going on?" I had a huge smile on my face.

He walked in. "I got the feeling you might enjoy eating in tonight. Don't worry. You'll still have your meal served. You won't have to do anything. I'll fix your plate and serve it to you. All you need to do is go back in your room, slip into something more comfortable, and let your man do all the work."

My eyebrows shifted up. "My man?" I giggled.

"Yeah, your man. Unless you don't want me to be yours."

"I didn't say that."

"Good, then go change." He gave me a soft peck on the lips.

By now he was in the kitchen pulling out Chinese food from China Palace. I hoped he had some Shrimp Egg Foo Young in that bag. I was on cloud nine. I now had a man and didn't have to get all dolled up to go out.

After stuffing ourselves with Chinese food, I'd had two helpings of Egg Foo Young and three egg rolls, we sat on the couch talking and laughing. "So now this event is over, maybe we'll have more time to hang out." He reached down and pulled my feet into his lap. I scooted around and laid back on the opposite end of the couch. If this brother wanted to rub my feet, I didn't want to disappoint him.

I told him I would definitely make time, but I still had a lot going on right now.

"I know you're always busy with the girls at the home. Are you referring to Angela and the mystery man? I told you if you could get me some information on the guy, I can have some friends check him out."

"It's not just that. I've been meaning to tell you something. I hope you don't think I come from a dysfunctional family." I don't know why I said that because I knew I came from a dysfunctional family.

He didn't miss a beat on the foot massage. "What is it? Sounds a little serious."

I took a deep breath. "I recently found out that I have twin brothers."

The massaging came to a sudden halt. Matthew's eyes narrowed as his brows crinkled together. "What do you mean? Your father had some children outside of the marriage?"

I chuckled. "I wish it were that simple. It seems my mother was pregnant with twin boys and my father made her give them up for adoption at birth." Now he looked as confused as I still was.

"Why'd your father want to give up his boys? I don't want to assume, but a few thoughts for why any man would want to give up his sons are coming to mind right now."

"I bet you my paycheck from this event none of your reasons would even come close." He waited patiently for the rest of the story. "My dad blackmailed my mother to give up their sons because he knew they'd be darker than I was and they'd grow up to be black men." Matthew turned his body towards me, staring at me as if he had to try to see the words that were coming from my mouth.

He paused for a minute, still having a confused look on his face. "Wow. Are you sure about this? Baby, I'm sorry. I've heard a lot of stories about a lot of different things, but…why don't you just start from the beginning and tell me how you found out this information so I can understand better."

I told him about the pictures in the closet and my mother's confession. I even told him I had hired a private investigator and he'd given me information on Jerome. I reminded him of where my parents came from and how it was back in the late sixties and early seventies. Also, how racist my grandparents were. As I sat there trying to explain this craziness, I became more disappointed in my mother. We came from a long line of survivors, people of great pride, that's whose blood was running through my veins. How could she go along with this nonsense without fighting? Children were the most precious gifts from God. How could any woman give them away because of their husband's fear of what might happen? What kind of woman was she? Tears began to fill my eyes as I questioned who I came from. Matthew pulled me to him. I rested my head in his lap until early morning. We got up and went to bed. That night brought us even closer.

Chapter Ten

"Wow, I see the Sheriff's Department isn't hurting from any budgetary cuts. Look at this place. This is a five star hotel," Libby said.

"Don't start no mess in here," Richard growled. "Just sit back and enjoy the evening. Everyone's a little touchy when it comes to budget topics."

"He must mean the first line people because the top executives never hurt as much as the worker bees," Libby mumbled to Marilyn.

"Here's our table." At the table, three other couples were seated. They all greeted each other with smiles and hellos. The women carried on with small talk about their children, some were in college, some in high school. One couple was around Richard and Marilyn's age with grown children. All of the other women had jobs outside of the home. They discussed the hectic lives they had trying to keep everything in order. Marilyn sat quietly listening to the other four women, including Libby adding to the conversation. One of the women, Mrs. Johnson, said, "Marilyn, you're so quiet. Why don't you jump on in here to this venting session?" They all giggled. The men were having their own private conversation about work, politics, and criminals as usual, but before Marilyn could answer Mrs. Johnson, she noticed Richard had slightly shifted his eyes over at her; as if to warn her to not participate in the cackling hen's conversation. That's what Richard usually referred to women who talked about their jobs, kids, social life – pretty much anything.

Marilyn caught the look and politely answered, "Well, our daughter is grown and I'm just a housewife."

The three women surveyed Marilyn with pity before another lady spoke, "Do you have any hobbies?"

"No, I don't. Keeping the house together and taking care of my husband is enough for me." She forced a weak half-crooked smile.

Mrs. Johnson said, "Well, you certainly keep yourself in shape. You look great."

"Thank you. I try." Marilyn gave a sigh of relief. She'd surely said the right thing to pass the test. Richard wouldn't be upset with her. She could rest tonight. On the other hand, she could see she'd pissed Libby off. She could see the look of daggers coming from the corner of Libby's eyes.

The tension was building at the table when Mrs. Johnson quickly said, "Marilyn, I think you're very lucky to be able to relax at home and not have to work and be a chauffer to teens all day. They're involved in so much, and the schools with their fundraisers keep the parents just as busy as the students." The women chimed in and began chatting amongst themselves again. The waiters finally got to their table with the salads, and the main course followed soon after that.

Everyone stuffed their mouths and couples chatted with each other for a while. Libby spoke quietly to Marilyn about some of her hobbies and tried to encourage her to get into something outside of the house because it would be good for her.

Richard leaned in towards Marilyn and Libby who sat on the opposite side of her. "Libby I'm warning you. Stay out of our business."

"What are you talking about? Seems like you're the one who's getting into our conversation over here. I'm simply talking to Marilyn about outside hobbies."

"She doesn't need outside hobbies. She's busy enough tending to the house." Richard said, trying to keep his huge voice to a minimum so that others couldn't hear him.

"Thank you for your concern, but I'm not interested. Let's just enjoy the evening."

After dessert was served, most of the sheriffs began to mingle and huddle with each other throughout the ballroom.

****

Richard spotted James at one of the nearby tables. As he walked towards him, James started walking his way and met him halfway. "Hey, James, how's it going?"

"Fine, sir. How are you and the missus?"

Richard rolled his eyes. "We're just fine."

"I noticed Brittney wasn't with you and Mrs. Adams."

"No, she had other plans. She had some big event earlier today and was tired."

"I ran into her and her boyfriend the other night in Westwood."

"Boyfriend? Why do you think he was her boyfriend?"

"Just the way they were interacting with each other. When I came over and introduced myself, he seemed a little overprotective. She said he was a parole officer, I think she said his name was Matthew."

Richard squinted. "What did he look like?"

"Oh he's about six-two, muscular, with a dark brown complexion." James knew his mention of Matthew's skin color would pierce Richard like a freshly sharpened knife.

As a lieutenant, Richard kept his ideas and emotions in check, but his close circle of friends knew he had an unjustified suspicion of most black men. Although James was not in this circle, he had learned of Richard's ideology through another detective in the station. No one felt he was racist...how could they? He was married to a black woman and loved his half-black daughter more than anything in the world.

Before he could finish his conversation with James, Richard noticed a man paying too much attention to Marilyn. She had a glowing smile, one he hadn't seen in years. Libby stood with them, but the man seemed more interested in Marilyn. As Richard walked closer, he recognized the gentleman, John Stokes. He never liked him and didn't even know why. He was a lieutenant at one of the Los Angeles stations. John was just about five feet ten inches tall and had a well-maintained body for a gentleman in his late fifties to early sixties. He looked like an older version of Idris Elba, with salt and pepper hair and had a way with the ladies. While still on the path to make it to his wife and sister to see what was so funny, Richard saw a small group of women gawking at John and commenting on his looks. Richard made his way to the three and stood beside Marilyn. Marilyn continued to laugh until she looked up at Richard. "Oh, hi, are we being too loud over here?" Her laugh quickly dissolved.

"Hey, Richard, right? How you doing, man? Do you know these lovely ladies?" John casually pointed at Marilyn and Libby.

"This is my wife." Richard pointed, slightly turning to Marilyn. "And this is my sister." He pointed at Libby.

"You're kidding. You mean this gorgeous woman is your wife?"

"Hey, I'm no horse's butt over here." Libby had a glowing personality and a contagious laugh. She was on the heavy side, but everything was in its proper place, as they'd say in the south. She was one of those women who couldn't tan to save her life, which left her pale white. She had piercing green eyes, rosy cheeks, and jet black hair, dyed of course.

"Certainly not. I meant both of you are gorgeous. I was just surprised this guy could convince such a jewel to marry him." Libby and John both laughed. The uneasiness from that comment was written all over Marilyn's face.

Richard chuckled. "Everybody wants to be a comedian around here, huh."

"Ah, come on, Dick, don't take it personal." John had a half smile.

"The name's Richard."

"Wow. I thought all you Richards liked being called Dicks." John laughed. "Lighten up." He turned to Libby and Marilyn. "So what do you ladies do?"

Libby promptly said, "I'm a school teacher. I teach junior high students."

John turned to her. "Well, you are affected as much as we are with all of these budget cuts. I'm so sick of this economy and the knuckleheads running it."

"What do you mean knuckleheads? You probably voted for him to be your president."

"Him? I know you're not trying to put all this on President Obama? This mess was here the first day he stepped into office. As a matter of fact, he had to roll up his pant legs to walk into the Oval office with all the crap Bush left. And what about your Governor Schwatzinigga, or whatever his name is?"

"Look, you two, let's not have a political war in here tonight." Libby waved her hands like a retreat banner.

"Anyway, I think it's about time we get going," Richard said.

"Man, it's still early." John said.

"Yeah, it's still early. What's your rush? Have a date with the television? I'm having a good time. I'm not ready to leave," Libby chided Richard.

"You can stay if you find someone willing to drive you all the way to Sherman Oaks area."

"I'm not too far from Sherman Oaks. I'll take you home if you want to stay. You can ask your brother here. I'm harmless." John grinned.

Libby turned to Marilyn. "Do you mind if I stay a little longer?"

"What are you asking her for? She's not in charge of you," Richard said.

"Being polite. I am her guest."

"You're my guest, both of you are guests."

"Whatever. I'll see you at home."

****

On the way home from the event, Richard reprimanded Marilyn. "I know you don't think John is interested in you. He flirts with anything and everything that wears a skirt and he's so disrespectful. Can you believe him? I should've punched him in the face. What do you think you were doing laughing all in his face like that? Did you forget you were a married woman?" Marilyn sat quietly listening to Richard rant and rave. "Oh, you can't talk now? You didn't seem to be having a problem opening your big mouth when John was talking to you."

Marilyn's eyes remained focused on the road ahead. "We were all just having a harmless conversation."

"You don't tell me what's harmless and what's not. I tell you. I didn't appreciate you embarrassing me like that in front of my men."

Marilyn's head snapped around to look at him. "Embarrass you? I can't believe you said that. You treat me more like your property than your wife and you say I embarrassed you?"

They pulled into the driveway, while the garage door was going up. Richard slammed on the brakes until the door had raised far enough up to clear the car before driving in. He slammed on the brakes again after entering the garage. He grabbed Marilyn's arm as she reached for the car door handle to get out of the car. Her eyes grew wide with fear. Richard grabbed her face with his other hand, forcing her to be face to face with him, "Don't you ever disrespect me like that again! I deserve better than that. I'm the one that has taken care of you all of these years. I'm the one who has lost everything over you, and you have the nerve to flirt with another man right in my face. How dare you? Do you think I'm going to take that from someone like you? I hope you don't let Libby and John get it into your head to think you can do better than me. Get out of the damn car!" Richard furiously shoved her against the car door.

Marilyn opened the door and ran into the house, allowing the door between the garage and the house to slam behind her. Richard chased after her. Tears flowed down Marilyn's cheeks. She heard the garage door slam as soon as she reached their bedroom. She turned around only to see Richard plunging towards her. He grabbed her again, this time by her dress around her neck and slung her on the king-sized bed. "You're just full of yourself tonight, aren't you? Who the hell do you think you are letting that door slam in my face? You think you're too good for your husband tonight? You're nothing. You're nothing!" He rammed her head into the bed with his hand and left her sobbing in their room.

****

About an hour later, Libby banged on the door. Richard opened the door. Libby burst in smiling and sashayed her way to the family room. Richard sat down in his huge worn chair.

"Where's Marilyn?" Libby asked.

"She's asleep," Richard grunted.

"Good. That gives us time to talk." Richard rolled his eyes. "Don't look like that. I know you love Marilyn, but do you remember how our daddy used to treat Momma? Well, I see so much of him in you."

Richard's eyes squinted. "The mere fact I am with Marilyn shows I'm nothing like Dad. Don't ever say I'm like him because we're total opposites."

Libby giggled. "On the contrary, you are more like Daddy than you care to admit." Libby sat on the end of the couch, close to his chair, and leaned towards him. "I think you have a lot of anger in you. You're hurt, confused, bitter, and, I believe, feeling very ashamed."

Richard turned to her. "Ashamed? I have nothing to be ashamed of. Everything I have ever done was what was best for my family."

"So you're still living behind that lie? Anyway, I'm not trying to bring up the past. I'm more concerned with what's going on now, right here in the present. You have a beautiful daughter who doesn't like you...no, let me rephrase that, can't stand the sight of you. That should bother you. You two used to be so close."

"It's that college that made her change. Women get too much education and money and then lose all respect for tradition and family."

"I can't believe you're sitting here saying that. You know that's a lie. Let's speak the truth here. Brittney doesn't like you because she sees how you treat her mother. Regardless of how much she loves you, Marilyn is her mother, and to be honest with you, you treat her like crap. You're always putting her down. I have personally heard you call her stupid in front of your daughter. You dismiss her like she's beneath you and her opinion doesn't matter. That's why your daughter thinks you're a racist. She knew Daddy was and you exhibit a lot of his characteristics. Come on, you're a smart man. You have to know this."

"Don't come into my house telling me how to run my family. I don't need to hear it right now."

"You need to hear this because you're losing your daughter. One day your wife might get a spine and leave you as well. Do you want that to happen?"

Richard's macho attitude diminished. "Have you ever been a certain way for so long you just don't know how or can't change? I am angry but not always at myself. I know I shouldn't feel this way but sometimes I see Princess and Marilyn laughing and talking together and I'm pissed off because I feel...I don't know, like it's just the two of them and I don't matter. Then I think of everything I gave up for her, for both of them, and I get angry. I know that's wrong because a man is supposed to take care of his family and sacrifice for them, but I gave up more than the average man. Loving her almost cost me my life. It did cost me everyone in my family, except for you, of course. I guess I am a monster sometimes." Richard seemed to be replying to himself. "You know I give her everything she wants. That woman has never wanted for anything. I've worked my butt off to make sure she and Brittney never went without."

"Sweetie, sometimes giving things and money isn't the best way to show your love for a person. You need to show kindness and respect. That respect you're always demand-ing. Being with you hasn't been all that easy for Marilyn, either. She went through her share of problems to stay with you, and as far as I'm concerned, is still suffering to stay by your side. Are you trying to punish her for your loss?"

"How could you even ask me that?"

"Easy. If you're comparing losses, don't forget about what Marilyn has lost. She's proven her devoted love to you year after year after year." Libby stood up. "I'm going to bed. I'll talk to you in the morning." She walked towards the hallway to the guest bedroom.

"Wait." Richard screeched as he jumped up to meet her. "Did John say anything about Marilyn? I mean was he trying to pump you for information about her?"

"What makes you think he wasn't interested in me, you old fool?" Libby snapped.

"Well, was he?"

"No. Believe it or not, he's just a very nice friendly guy. He was a perfect gentleman. Marilyn is a beautiful woman. One day she's going to get fed up with being treated like a freakin' doormat Good night."

Chapter Eleven

There's no rest for the weary, I guess. Ms. Cooper called me the next morning about that strange man who'd been sneaking around seeing Angela. The man was too old to be involved with a sixteen year old and Angela wouldn't talk to anyone about him. I was going to have to get some information about him so I could at least have Matthew check him out. He was careful to never come in the house or even come close to the front door.

I arrived at the house at ten thirty. The ladies were preparing to go to eleven o'clock church service. I told Ms. Cooper I wanted to spend some time with Angela so she wouldn't be attending services with them that morning.

I walked upstairs and tapped on Angela's door. "Come in."

I opened the door and stepped in and sat at the foot of her bed as she crimped the last few curls on her long ash brown hair. "I'd like for us to spend a little time together this morning, if that's okay with you."

Angela stopped fussing with her hair and looked at me through the mirror like a frightened child. "Why? Did I do something wrong?"

"Not at all. I just want to talk to you. Did you eat this morning?"

"No. I got up too late so I just had some juice."

"Well, why don't we go to brunch. Denny's or IHOP?"

"IHOP." Angela smiled.

Fifteen minutes later we were sitting in IHOP. I could tell getting information out of her was going to be like pulling teeth. "Remember I told you that you could always talk to me about anything? I want you to know you can trust me. I only want to help take care of you and your unborn baby." The waiter interrupted to take our orders. Angela definitely ate for two. She ordered the All-You-Can-Eat pancake special with eggs, bacon, and sausage.

I jumped right back in to the conversation as soon as the waiter left. "Do you understand you do not and should not have to pay for raising this child alone? The father of the child should be held responsible for his part. I know you told me you two were not in a relationship but he..."

"Can we please not talk about this?"

"All right. Then let's talk about that man we've seen you talking to a few times since you moved into Ebony Eyes."

She looked surprised and frightened at the same time. "Who is he and why doesn't he just come in to visit you? Why the secrecy? He looks kind of old." She shifted side to side, crossing her legs, then uncrossing them. Her breathing became deeper and stronger. I didn't want to cause her to go into early labor. Her face became pale and flushed.

"He's just some guy," she finally said.

"No, he's not just some guy. Is he your baby's father?"

"No." Angela practically screamed with panic. She was clearly insulted by the question. Her face wrinkled up in disgust.

"I'm not trying to upset you but I need to know who this guy is and why every time he comes around you seem to have a bad night. Is he bothering you? If you've been with this guy sexually, you're not to blame. He is. Older men convince girls like you they care just to get into their pants and to keep their secrets. If you've gotten caught up in all this, it's not your fault. You're the victim."

"You think you know everything. You don't know anything about me. I don't go around having sex with men or boys."

"Then why don't you tell me about you? I'm listening." She began to cry. The food came and we both took a short break to eat. She ate slowly. I could tell she wanted to share something with me but was still scared. I broke the silence. "How do you and your mother get along?"

"My mom thinks I'm a slut." She fought back the tears.

I was shocked to hear her say that so bluntly. "I'm sure she doesn't think that. You just made a mistake. She's probably upset and still needs time to get used to the fact

103

that her baby is having a baby. I read your file. It says you were a very good student. You averaged A's and B's all the way up until the tenth grade. That's when you began hanging out, missing school, and getting into trouble. What happened? I want to hear your side of the story."

"My mom acted as if she didn't need me anymore when she got her new boyfriend. We used to do everything together. I'm the oldest and she always said she could trust me to take care of my little brother and sister. I used to take care of them, but they're just a few years under me. They're eleven and thirteen. My mom knew I was responsible. She always said I was a good daughter. We used to take care of our family together."

"What happened?" I asked.

"He came in and acted like he owned the place. Momma allowed him to make rules, and they were always gone. She never had anytime for us. That's when I started hanging out with my friend, Gretchen, and her older brother. I stayed with them a lot. They were like my second family." Her eyes filled with tears again. "We went everywhere together. One day, me and my mom got into a big argument because I wasn't coming home everyday after school to make sure my brother and sister were getting their homework done. I was going out on the weekends, staying out past my curfew. She came down on me real hard about what I was supposed to be doing for my brother and sister, and I yelled back telling her they were her children not mine." She tried to keep the tears off her face by wiping, but she couldn't wipe fast enough. "As I ran out the door, I saw Bryan and Tasha standing at the door crying. I wanted to tell them I loved them, but I was so angry I didn't stop to say anything to them."

I wanted to ask her if that was when she got involved with the father, but she was finally trusting me enough to open up. I didn't dare push it. I waited and allowed her to take her own time and tell me the whole story. I was willing to sit with her all day if that's what it took to get to the mystery man.

Angela stared into space. "I started drinking every once in a while, but I never slept around. I'm not a slut." She looked up at me. "I was a virgin."

I reached for her hand. "It's okay." *This is getting way too heavy to continue in IHOP.* I waived to our waiter for the check. We hopped up, paid the check, and rushed out to the parking lot. There was a quiet little neighborhood behind the parking lot so I suggested we take a walk. I placed my hand around her shoulders and asked her to finish telling me how she ended up at Ebony Eyes.

"Ms. Adams, I'm not fast. He was my best friend. I trusted him. He was like my big brother, well sort of. We were at this party. I'd had a lot to drink so we left and went back to his house because I was sleepy. When we got there, we went to his room. He gave me some more to drink, and he started playing music and dancing. I remember dancing with him. We always danced together so it wasn't a big deal. Then he started kissing me, and at first I kissed him back. I guess I had a little crush on him, but when he started feeling on my breast, I pushed him back. He kept kissing me and we were on the bed. He started unbuttoning my pants. I said "No," but he kept doing it. I was pushing him, but he was too heavy for me. I finally just stopped fighting him and let him..."

We stopped and I held her while she continued sobbing. "Baby, you were raped. Sex without consent is rape. He should be in jail."

"No." Angela pushed away from me. "You can't tell anyone. You can't call the police. He didn't mean it. He's my friend. We were both drunk. It's not his fault."

"Shhh. It's all right. Don't get yourself so worked up. We'll work this out together, okay?" She shook her head yes. "Did you tell your mother what happened?"

"I tried, but she didn't want to hear anything I had to say. She just kept saying she didn't think she'd raised a girl like me. That I was just fast and out of control. She didn't want to hear anything I had to say. It was easier to start looking for somewhere to place me so I wouldn't mess up things between her and her boyfriend."

"So Gretchen's older brother is your baby's father?"

"I didn't say that!" She pulled away and vanished into that little scared girl again. I saw the distrust return in her eyes.

"Angela, you can trust me. I'm not going to talk to anyone about this without your permission, all right?"

"Okay."

"You still haven't told me who that man who keeps hanging around the building is."

"He's just a friend. I told him what happened and he comes by to check on me. That's all."

I knew I wasn't getting anything else out of her right now. "Let's go back to the car and get you home."

When we returned, Ms. Cooper and Ms. Wilma were monitoring the ladies in the recreation room. I said good-bye to Angela and reassured her I wouldn't speak to anyone about her situation until we spoke again. She nodded and ran to her room. Before I left, I told Ms. Cooper and Ms. Wilma to call me immediately if that guy came around or if Angela left the house.

Chapter Twelve

M onday morning, I decided to call Mr. Benson to take him up on his offer. It was a holiday weekend but he told me he'd be in the office. He'd offered to go with me to meet Jerome. I was so nervous. I had butterflies in my stomach with the thought of meeting this stranger. Although we shared the same blood, we were total strangers. I picked up the phone and dialed. "Hello, Mr. Benson, it's me, Brittney Adams."

"How are you, Ms. Adams?"

"Ok, I guess. I'm calling because I'm ready to take you up on your offer."

"All right. Let me get your file. Hold on please."

"Sure."

There was a brief pause. The sound of shuffling folders came through the phone. "I have some more news for you. I checked out the last known address for Jaden. He's no longer living there, but I did find out he's on probation. I'm just waiting on a phone call to find out his probation officer's name. Once I get in touch with him, I'll certainly be able to retrieve Jaden's new location. He's in the Los Angeles area."

"That's great!! What do you think I should do? Wait until you find him first since he's so close? Or go ahead with the plans to meet Jerome? I'm so excited and frightened to death at the same time."

"It's up to you, Ms. Adams, but I'd recommend contacting Jerome first. Only because he seems more together and has the resources to check out your story and who you are so he knows this isn't some kind of hoax. He's a professional, responsible man. I'm sorry to say, but your other brother Jaden appears to be somewhat of a loose cannon."

"I understand. Where do we start? I'm ready."

"How soon do you want to make that trip?"

"As soon as possible. Can you go this week?"

"Wow, you mean business, don't you?" Mr. Benson said.

"Yes. I need to meet him and tell him who he is." A sudden thought came to mind. He might not want to know who he is, but I pushed that thought right out of my mind.

"Let me check my schedule. I'll get back to you later today."

"I'll wait to hear from you. Good-bye, Mr. Benson."

I couldn't believe by the end of the week I might have met one of my brothers. I didn't want to tell Mom until I'd met him. I immediately called Matthew to tell him what was happening. We were in a real relationship and it felt good. "Hey you, how you doing?"

"I'm good, baby. What's going on with you today?"

"A lot. I just got off the phone with Mr. Benson. We're planning a trip to Maryland to meet my brother Jerome."

"Wow! You sure you're ready to do this?"

"Absolutely."

"Good. Do you want some company?"

"No, I think I need to do this on my own. I mean, Mr. Benson is going to accompany me and speak with Jerome first so it's not a total shock for him to see me. I'm not sure how all this works, but I'll be just fine. Besides, I have something else I need you to do for me."

"You know I'll do pretty much anything for you so shoot, what is it?"

"Ahhh! Thanks. You're so sweet. I found out what happened to Angela. She was raped but is still trying to protect the person that did it. I told Ms. Cooper and Ms. Wilma to contact me if either of them spot our mystery man again. I'm still trying to connect the dots. If you're available when they call, I'd like to high-tail it over there and follow him to see if he'll lead us to the rapist." Matthew and I both lived only about fifteen minutes away from the home but in opposite directions. He lived in the Los Feliz area in a gorgeous home his parents left for him. His mom passed about three years ago then a year later his father died.

Matthew was their only child so there was no family drama when it came to the possessions they left behind.

"What? Are you crazy? You don't know what type of people you're dealing with. You need to report this to the police or at least a social worker."

"I can't. Not now. I promised Angela I wouldn't tell anyone until we spoke again. Please come with me."

"Of course I'll come with you. I'm not going to let you go off following some guy to God only knows where by yourself. Who do you think you are anyway, Christie Love?"

"Oh, you remember that show? She was bad, huh?"

"Brittney, promise me you won't do anything or play detective without me."

"I won't. That's why I'm telling you. I just want to get the whole story before I confront her again." Her phone beeped. Caller ID showed Ebony Eyes. "Matthew, hold on. It's Ebony Eyes on the other line." I clicked over. "Hello."

"He's baaaack," Ms. Wilma said quietly. "She said she was going to take a walk. I went to the upstairs bedroom to peek out of the window and I could see her across the street down by the corner. He walked up about three minutes after she got there."

"Thanks. Talk to you later, bye." I clicked back to Matthew. "How soon can you get there? The guy just returned."

"I can get there in about fifteen minutes. Do you want me to get you first?"

"No. No time for that. I'll meet you there, but meet me around the corner at St. Andrews and Harold Way."

"Will do, but don't follow him by yourself if he leaves before I get there."

"Then make sure you get there before he leaves. Bye." I snatched my purse and keys, then jetted out the door. I could make it to Ebony Eyes in about ten minutes if there were no police around and since it was a holiday there'd be little to no traffic but probably police around. Who was I kidding? That was doing about eighty mph which was my norm if traffic allowed. I could probably push it to eighty-five and get there in seven minutes.

I arrived at our meeting location in eleven minutes flat. I spotted Angela and the man on the corner. She was leaning up against an old car that looked like a blue Saturn. That loud electric blue so it'd be easy to follow. Angela waived her hands, shaking her head as if in disagreement with whatever he was saying. I hoped Matthew would get here soon, because when he moved, I'd move. I wished I had the good sense to bring my binoculars so I could see his face better. With that hood on, it probably wouldn't make a difference anyway. He looked suspicious. Why did he have a hood on as warm as it was? He was really trying to convince her of something. I heard a car pull up behind me. I looked back and saw Matthew. Good. I didn't want to do this alone. He jumped out of his pearl white Lexus, but I quickly removed my keys from the ignition and waved for him to stay put. He got back in his car. I ran to the passenger side.

"Hi. I think it's best to follow him in your car. He may have seen mine parked in the driveway before and I don't want to take any chances." Angela began walking towards the house. The man got back in his car. He drove down the street right in front of us. We took off after him.

"I'll get close enough for you to get the license plate." I grabbed a baseball hat from the backseat and put it on to help disguise myself. I felt very Christie Loveish. I wrote down the license plate as we continued following for about twenty minutes. We were on Sunset Blvd. heading east towards Vermont. We passed Kaiser Permanente Hospital on the left. He made a right turn on Vermont. We continued traveling on it for a couple of blocks before he made another right turn on a small side street. Then another right on the second street and he finally parked in front of some run-down apartments on a side street. I wrote the address down.

"Well, aren't you going to park?"

"No. We don't know what's in there. You have enough information on this dude already. We can run the plates and match them with this address. You don't need the apartment number."

"I'd like to go in and talk to him. That's the only way to get to the bottom of this."

"No. That's the way you get your crazy butt shot. You don't have Daddy's police force behind you. These people around here don't know you're Lieutenant Daddy's little girl, and from the looks of some of these people, they wouldn't care anyway."

I didn't want to admit it, but I knew he was right. "Okay. Let's go back empty-handed." Matthew shook his head and made a u-turn and sped off.

The next morning, Matthew called with the name of the registered owner of the car which matched the address we followed him to. We were no closer today to finding out who he was than we were last week. The car was registered to a Belinda Hughes. "Who the heck is she?"

"I don't know, but I've got a pretty heavy day today, so we'll have to discuss this later. Promise me you won't do anything without me today."

"Promise."

"Talk to you later. Bye."

"Bye and thank you."

Later, I chased down some scrambled eggs with grape-fruit juice and headed for Bally's. I needed to work out for about 3 hours to clear my head. Before I hit the door, the phone rang. "Hello."

"Hello, Ms. Adams, this is Mr. Benson."

"Oh hi, I wasn't expecting a call so soon. Is everything okay? Anything new?"

"Not exactly. I wanted to let you know I cleared my schedule for Thursday through Saturday. Is that too soon for you to meet your brother?"

There was a big lump in my throat. The palms of my hands were sweaty. "No. It's not too soon." I sat down. I lied, it was too soon. I was moving too fast. I wasn't ready. Fears of him hating me consumed my mind.

"Do you have time to meet with me either today or to-morrow to go over the details of the trip?" My entire body trembled. "Ms. Adams?"

"Yes. I'm here. Ummm, today would be fine. What time?"

"Can you come to my office around one thirty?"

"Sure. I'll be there."

"See you then."

"Thank you, bye." I still had time to get in a good workout and boy, did I need one.

I arrived at Mr. Benson's at exactly one twenty-five and sat in my car for a minute to gather myself. I couldn't believe I was about to make arrangements to meet my brother. What I most worried about was if he'd resent me because I grew up with Mom and Dad and he was tossed from place to place. I opened the door slowly, ignoring the butterflies floating around in my stomach and entered the tall building. The glass doors felt extremely heavy, but it could have been my normal strength had been diminished due to worry, guilt, and shame. Why was I ashamed? I didn't give him away. I didn't allow my husband to throw away my babies without a fight. I did none of those things but somehow I felt just as responsible.

I finally reached suite two-zero-seven. Marching up to the receptionist, I introduced myself. "Hi. I'm Brittney Adams, here to see Mr. Benson."

"Please sign in and have a seat." I slid the clipboard closer to her after I signed my name.

I liked meeting in the restaurant better. This was way too formal for me. I heard the receptionist telling Mr. Benson I was there.

"Ms. Adams, Mr. Benson is ready to see you now. Go through this door and make a quick left. His office is the first door on the right."

"Thank you." My legs struggled to hold my body upright. When I reached his door, I knocked softly. Secretly I hoped he wouldn't hear me and I'd have to leave and come back another day. "Hello, Mr. Benson."

He bounced up and extended his hand out to me. "Hello, Ms. Adams, please have a seat." I shook his hand and immediately sat down. His office was really nice. Oversized plush leather chairs and a cherry wood veneer desk with matching credenza. This must be a big business, I thought. "I have a surprise for you."

He was smiling so I guessed this was a good surprise he was about to lay on me. "Surprise?"

"Yes. Then again you're so resourceful, you might have already gotten this yourself. Or at least one of them.

Now I was dying to know his surprise. "What is it?"

He opened his right desk drawer and pulled out a manila folder. He opened the folder and handed me a picture. "This is your brother Jerome."

Tears instantly filled my eyes. For a moment I couldn't breathe. I'd seen the pictures of him as a child, but now he was a real person in my hands. In a couple of days I'd be face to face with this stranger I was beginning to have feelings for. I stared at the photo for a few minutes forgetting there was someone else in the room. I heard Mr. Benson clear his throat, I guess to get my attention. The man in the picture had the same skin color as my mother, a beautiful coffee brown. His skin was silky smooth and he had a cheerful disposition. He looked confident and very satisfied with life. Suddenly, I was startled.

"Ms. Adams?"

"Yes?" I had slipped away for a few seconds. I hoped he hadn't said something earlier.

116

"I have another picture for you. This one may not be too pleasant to look at but it's all I have. It's a picture of your brother Jaden. It's his mug shot."

My hand quivered as I reached for the picture. The two men looked alike but totally different. Jaden's picture was disheartening; he looked dejected. His eyes were empty but familiar; it was the same emptiness I'd seen in my mother's eyes. His face was unshaven, hair uncombed; he looked hopeless. I felt pity for him. I didn't understand this. Jaden was the one that grew up in the two parent middle income family home. What happened? Everything felt backwards. I was meeting Jerome possibly this week but Jaden was the one that needed me. My thought instantly was to save and protect him. But from who? Himself? Or the world? I could no longer hold the tears back, looking at Jaden. I felt them roll down my cheeks tracing my chin and dropping inches from Jaden's face. I snapped back when Mr. Benson handed me a tissue. I wiped my face and apologized. For what, I didn't know.

"It's all right. I understand."

How could he understand? Had he been denied the right of a union between any of his siblings? Had he grown up with the pain of loving and hating his father at the same time? Had he watched his mother endure constant verbal abuse from someone who supposedly loved her? Was he the one sitting in a private detective's office looking down at his younger brother who obviously needed him long before now? No, I don't think he understood but it was nice of him to be empathetic to my situation. "What's the next step?" I asked with a calmness that surprised me.

"I'm going to call Jerome and tell him about the circumstances and see if he's willing to meet with us this week."

I almost fell out of my chair. The calmness vanished as fast as it had come. My eyes must have grown larger than a fifty-cent piece. "Right now?" My entire body shook with fear, joy, excitement, doubt, sadness; I was on an emotional roller coaster. "What do I say to him over the phone?" I was in a full-blown panic.

"Hold on a minute. I didn't say you'd call him. I said I'd call. I'm going to tell him about you and ask if I can bring you to visit him this week. Remember, he needs time to process this as well. I'm not going to even let him know you're sitting with me right now. As a matter of fact, maybe you'd be more comfortable waiting in the receptionist area."

"No," I blurted. "I'd rather stay here. I won't make a sound."

"Good." Mr. Benson removed another sheet of paper from the same folder and began punching in the numbers on his phone. "Hello, I'm Edward Benson, calling from California. Is Mr. Jerome Roclin available?" Mr. Benson's brow raised then he sighed with relief and a smile spread on his face so I guessed Jerome was available. "Hello, Mr. Roclin, I'm Edward Benson, a private investigator, from California."

For fifteen minutes I heard Mr. Benson tell my brother about me in very terse detail. He mostly answered Jerome's questions. I guess Jerome felt comfortable enough to meet me since Mr. Benson knew of almost all of the foster homes he grew up in. Mr. Benson made an appointment to meet him this Thursday at four o'clock. In just two days, I'd meet one of my brothers.

Chapter Thirteen

"Jaden, is that you?" Jaden still had a key to the house against his father's better judgment.

"Yeah, Mom." Jaden followed Mrs. Patterson's voice to the utility room near the garage. Mrs. Patterson continued loading clothes into the dryer. "Hey, Mom." Mrs. Patterson straightened up and gave her son a warm embrace.

"Hi, Jaden. I haven't seen you in a while. Is everything all right?" She asked suspiciously.

"Dang, Mom. Can't I just come by to say 'Hi' without you getting all suspicious?"

Mrs. Patterson waved her hands up in surrender. "Ok, but you know we don't usually see you unless you're in some kind of trouble or you need something..."

"Thanks, Mom. Maybe I don't come around much because your husband has made it clear he doesn't want me around." Jaden lifted the basket of clothes filled with clean laundry and began walking into the family room where his mom usually sat in front of their huge fifty-two inch flat screen television. She followed and sat in the corner of the love seat. Jaden placed the basket in front of her and she began her routine.

Barbara Patterson and her husband Donald both worked full-time jobs for as long as Jaden could remember. They lived comfortably. Jaden was the only child, used to getting mostly what he wanted and everything he needed.

"So, Jaden, have you found a job yet?"

"I told you I work almost every day." He held his head upright and boasted, "I get assignments from Labor Ready at least four times a week."

"I meant a steady full-time job, Jaden. I mean you can't really take care of yourself with temporary assignments. You need something permanent just to handle the bare necessities." Barbara dropped the pillowcase she folded into her lap. "I know you're trying, but you really need to go back to school to get a trade or something. It's hard trying to make ends meet even with a full-time job. You're thirty-two years old and…"

"Mom, you don't need to remind me how old I am and what I don't have and what I haven't accomplished. I'm very much aware of all that. You and Dad remind me of it all the time. Thank you." The pride he had felt seconds ago had faded.

Barbara took in a long breath, glaring at Jaden. "Are you hungry? There's plenty of food in the fridge."

Jaden hesitated. He didn't want to receive any charity from his parents, but the hunger pangs in his stomach convinced him otherwise.

****

He grew up in a loving environment. Both parents worked hard to give him everything he needed to grow up and be a successful, responsible, contributing adult to society.

During the first year of high school, Jaden's behavior began to change. He'd been an "A and B" student up to the ninth grade. He was respectful towards his parents. They had family gatherings often and everyone spoke highly of him.

The boys in the neighborhood he grew up with began teasing him, calling him a momma's boy, a square. All the neighborhood kids poked fun at each other, but this particular day was a little different. One of his friends said, "I don't think you're fully black, that's why you act the way you do. I think your momma has too much of that white blood in her. That's why your family acts like the freakin' Cleavers." Although they were all friends, the boys and girls laughed way too hard at this particular joke. Jaden already felt like he had to prove himself to fit in because his mother was high-yellow. Most people thought she was mixed with white but both of her parents were black.

Most of his friends had already started smoking cigarettes in junior high, but Jaden had avoided that habit. He still hung with his friends because he knew in spite of the joking they all had each other's back. Going to a new school where they were the scrubs on the campus, they vowed to stick together. But his friend Carl warned him he had to toughen up a bit. With the pressure from his friends and being in a new school, Jaden began missing curfew, hanging out with his friends more, and smoking weed. His grades dropped dramatically. He barely passed most of his classes. His parents went to the school countless times due to his behavior.

After a call from the school's dean one day, Mr. Patterson yelled at the top of his lungs about how tired he was of Jaden's attitude. Jaden hadn't come home from school yet. Mrs. Patterson was finally able to make her husband calm down agreeing to sit quietly and figure out a plan to get their son back on track.

"Sweetheart, he's just going through growing pains. All kids do, some worse than others." Mrs. Patterson sat on the bed next to him stroking his shoulders.

"If anyone is going through growing pains, it's us." Mr. Patterson growled. Then he dropped his head in his hands. "I did everything right. Everything I was supposed to do as a father. How did this happen?"

"Donald, don't blame yourself. He's just going through some changes. This isn't our fault. Maybe we need to think about sending him away to an all boys' school or one of those military academies?"

During Mr. Patterson's outrage, Jaden entered the house, but they didn't hear him. Jaden's room was next to theirs and he listened in on his parent's heartfelt conversation on what they should do with him.

"Donald, we need to do whatever it takes to get him back on track. We know he's a good boy."

"Do we really know that for sure?"

Mrs. Patterson looked puzzled. "Do we know what for sure?"

"Do we know he's a good boy? Maybe he's not. Maybe he's got bad genes. I mean, we really don't know anything about his real parents. All we know is that they didn't want him. His mother died shortly after giving birth. His father didn't want to have anything to do with him. Maybe he knew something we didn't." They were both startled by their son's voice coming from behind them.

They twisted around to find Jaden standing near the door. "NO!" The wells of his eyes filled quickly as he stood in the doorway shaking his head, perplexed at what he'd just heard. "You're not my parents?"

"Oh My God!" Mrs. Patterson hopped up and ran towards Jaden. She wrapped her arms around him and buried her head in his chest weeping. "I'm so sorry you had to hear it like this."

Jaden stood cemented to the floor, standing already five feet nine inches tall at age fifteen, although the revelation made him feel small, with a sorrowful bowed head. He didn't utter another word. His eyes were fixated on his father who stood across the room glaring back at him, seemingly trying to find the words to comfort his son.

Mr. Patterson broke the silence. "We need to sit down and talk."

Mrs. Patterson finally looked up at Jaden then back at her husband. "Yes, we need to sit down and talk." She grasped Jaden's hand and gestured. "Come sit down."

Jaden was still focused on his father before he snapped from his trance. "I need some air." He turned and ran down the stairs.

Mrs. Patterson screamed, "No, Jaden!" following behind him.

"Let him go." Mr. Patterson yelled from the top of the stairs. "He needs some time."

Jaden stood at the opened door glancing back at his father before walking out.

Mr. Patterson trotted down the stairs embracing his wife, feeling responsible for what happened. "He'll be all right." He said.

Jaden didn't return home that night. His mother paced the floor all night worrying, calling most of his friends to see if anyone had seen him. His closest buddies hadn't heard from him. The next morning they received a call from the police department stating their son was being held for burglary. This was the first of many bouts with the law.

****

Jaden stared into the refrigerator scanning all the options to fill his hunger. He leaned in when he spotted a plate of fried chicken, then noticed a container with candied yams. His juices began to flow because he knew his mom would definitely have some cabbage or collard greens to accompany the yams. Still shuffling items around, he spied the cabbage. With cabbage in the fridge, the cornbread couldn't be too far behind. He placed the goodies on the counter, retrieved a plate from the cabinet, and began loading the meal onto his plate. He placed the food in the microwave and closed the door, but not before ripping a paper towel from the spindle to place over the food to avoid food explosions. He slammed the door and selected two minutes.

Jaden's parents had lived in the same house for the past twenty years. They remodeled the kitchen and bathrooms. The kitchen had a nice island with black granite counter-tops, all new cabinetry, and all stainless steel appliances. Jaden leaned back against the counter with his arms folded, watching his delicious meal swirling around in the micro-wave. At that second, he didn't have a care in the world except the anticipation of enjoying the delectable meal he'd be diving into in about forty-five more seconds.

A loud noise from behind shook him out of his spell. He twisted his body halfway and then fully, facing his father.

"You can't come by here to visit your mother or me, but you can surely make your way here when you get hungry, huh?"

Mrs. Patterson bolted from the family room when she heard her husband's voice. She didn't expect him home for at least another two hours. "He didn't ask for anything, I offered him some food."

Her husband ignored her. "What do you need, money? A place to stay for a few days? I'm getting fed up with this." He stood on the opposite side of the island pointing his finger while Mrs. Patterson stood at his side trying to pull his arm down and quiet him.

"Please stop being so accusatory. Look at him. God knows he needs to eat something decent. He looks pitiful. Look at your son's face. He has dark circles around his eyes, his cheeks are sunken in like a…"

"A crackhead?"

Just then, the microwave went off with a loud "bing" noise. "I was going to say like a cancer patient." Mrs. Patterson looked at Jaden pitifully. "Please eat your food."

Jaden stared at his father. "I just lost my appetite." He walked around the island and kissed his mother on her cheek. "Good-bye, Mom." Jaden gave a sharp look at his father. "Good seeing you again, Donald." He walked out of the kitchen and through the front door, mumbling under his breath, "I'm never coming to this place again.

Chapter Fourteen

I called Adrienne as soon as I woke up. I had to tell her what was about to happen. I still couldn't believe I was going to meet my brother. We decided to meet for lunch at the Grand Luxe at the Beverly Center. The image of Jaden had been tattooed into my brain. That man looked so lost. He'd been right here in the same county as me for years. I could have bumped into him and wouldn't have known he was my brother. I could've met him and started dating him. I'd dated plenty of losers back in the day. *Oh My God!* I just referred to my own brother as a loser. I needed to chill out. While still in bed, I called to check on the ladies at Ebony Eyes.

"Hello, Ms. Wilma, how's everything going over there this morning? Everyone get off to school?"

"Yes. Things were so smooth this morning it felt a little eerie. No problems, no issues. What a blessing."

"Great. Good to hear that. I'll probably drop by late this evening, and will be going out of town tomorrow, so let's cross our fingers everything remains calm until I return. I'll see you and Ms. Cooper later."

"See you then. You have a good day."

"Thanks, you do the same."

I called Mom, but I couldn't bear to face her this week and definitely didn't want to see Dad's face. After a short conversation with Mom and hearing the good news from Ebony Eyes, the adrenaline began flowing again. I jumped out of bed, showered, and dashed into the kitchen. I was starving but didn't want to eat much since I was meeting Adrienne in a few hours. I grabbed a glass from the cabinet, opened the refrigerator, hoping I had at least enough orange juice for one glass. I did. Sitting at the breakfast bar I grabbed a pen and notepad and began jotting down answers to possible questions Jerome might ask.

I arrived at the Beverly Center, parked on the third floor near Bloomingdales, and rushed in, barely making it on time. Adrienne was a stickler for promptness and always scolded me about my tardiness. Not this time. I walked in exactly one minute before twelve. YES! I did it. I caught myself having to hold down my balled fist from rising as if I'd just won a relay race. "I beat Lady Promptness today," I mumbled to myself as I proudly walked up to the counter. "Hi, I'm expecting another person in my party…"

"Oh, are you with Adrienne Hampton?" She was way too cheery.

"Yes." I was baffled.

"Come this way." We took a few steps and wouldn't you know it? Adrienne sat comfortably in a booth waving at me. She was already sipping on her Pepsi.

Adrienne stood up and met me with a big hug. She got me again. "Hey, girl, I see you arrived on time for a change. I told her I wanted to be seated because there was no telling what time you'd get here." She laughed her infectious laugh. We scooted into the booth, wiggling until we closed the gap between us.

"Ok, but I was on time. No one said anything about arriving early."

"Girl, I know. I'm just joking with you. So, tell me what's going on."

Adrienne and I sat there for hours eating and talking. I told her everything but mainly spilled my guts about how I felt about my father. When I was growing up, I thought my Dad was the best in the world. I didn't witness him treating Mom badly or, I should say, I didn't realize how he was treating her until my early teens. I think that's when I noticed how he spoke to her and his tone. He chastised her as if she were his child, too. Then I started noticing the way she had to get permission from him for anything she wanted to do. This wasn't like talking things over out of respect for a marriage, it was a parent-child relationship. My father was old fashioned. I know he was raised a certain way so a lot of his actions came from that but something changed. Now looking back, I think it was around the time Grandpa Adams died.

I released a deep sigh. "I know my father used to love my mother. He wasn't always like this. Something clicked and the occasional moody, disrespectful attitude I saw seemed to escalate daily. Now he makes me just sick to look at him."

Adrienne took my hand. "When all this is over and everything is out in the open, you're going to have to deal with these feelings you have for your father because this isn't healthy for you. I know he did a horrible thing…"

I interrupted, "And continues to do and say horrible things. Adrienne, what you don't understand is there's so much damage that's been done. Verbal abuse tears you down spiritually, emotionally, and physically. What's even worse is the abused victims sometimes become oblivious to what's happening to them. They learn to live with it, expect it, and welcome it as if it's confirmation of how dedicated and strong they are to endure it. Sometimes the abused explodes and snaps. Those are the ones you end up seeing on the news. I think my father is that abuser."

"Sweetie, I know, but what I'm saying is, you're going to have to have a long talk with your father so you're not filled with hatred. You know what the Bible says about forgiveness…"

"Girl, please, don't start talking to me about what thus said the Lord. You know I'm not into that."

"Well, you need to get into that. You need Jesus. We all do." She giggled.

Church was the one thing Adrienne and I totally disagreed on. She was a believer and I wasn't. At least not a believer of organized religion. I believed in God. Although I grew up in the church, every Sunday I began noticing things that weren't quite right. The adults that seemed to act the most religious were gossiping and being nasty towards one another all the time. What really turned me away was when I was around eighteen one of the married young ministers kept eyeing me. He'd make comments I felt were inappropriate, but I was young so I just avoided him. Months later I found out he was sleeping with another young woman in the church. His wife sat on the second pew on the right side of the building while his mistress sat on about the fifth pew on the left side of the building. That was too much. About two years after that, I found out my aunt Libby was having an affair with her minister. No one could tell me anything about going to church after that. To me it was just a big corrupt business and a bigger joke.

"Please, let's not talk about God, Jesus, or religion today. I have way too much on my mind right now. My brothers have to be my main focus now."

"Girl, that's when you need to get on your knees and have a little talk with Jesus. I understand what you're saying, but you need to focus on Christ not the people in the church. The devil shows up every where. It's his plan to keep you and others from seeking God and building a relationship with Him. I won't go there today, but we are going to have to talk about this again. Do you need me to go with you? You know I'll do anything for you."

"Thanks, but I think I'm going to do this on my own. Matthew offered to go, too." I smiled.

"You and Matthew are kinda tight, huh?"

I had a wide grin that probably made me look like a foolish teen because I flashed all my teeth. "Yeah, we're kinda tight. He's really nice and, more importantly, very dependable." We laughed and gave each other high fives.

"That's what I'm talking about. A brother you can depend on. Girl, I ain't mad at you." Adrienne laughed. "Why don't you let him go with you and make a little romantic weekend out of it?"

"That's exactly why I don't want him to come. Romance will be the last thing on my mind. Besides, I want to be open in case Jerome wants to spend some time with me."

We finally left the Grand Luxe around three forty-five. Matthew had called twice while I was there. I'd promised to call when I was headed home. I called Ms Cooper to let her know I wouldn't get over there that evening – I had too much to do. Everything was still going well at Ebony Eyes. I felt comfortable missing one day.

A couple of hours later, I called Mom. She asked why I hadn't been to see her. I had made a habit of visiting at least every couple of days. I hadn't seen her since the fashion show on Saturday. I used that as an excuse. Since I'd been so busy, I'd put aside other things I needed to attend to. I explained I needed to meet with a possible client out of state so I wouldn't see her until probably Sunday, but I would call her every day. I knew she wasn't really buying my story because it wasn't like me not to squeeze ten or twenty minutes into a hectic day to see my mom. I pretended to be in a rush, told her I loved her, and got off the phone before she could make me feel any more guilty than I was already feeling.

In another hour, Matthew would be arriving, so I decided to start packing. I hopped on the computer to check the weather forecast. I felt this desire to impress Jerome. I wanted to be perfect. He was my brother, the attorney, sophisticated and well educated. I was still feeling ashamed. I had the weight of the world on my shoulders, but why? I needed a glass of wine to calm myself down. The white wine I found shoved in the back of the refrigerator did the trick.

Matthew and I talked all night. He was an excellent listener. I felt like such a wimp; like a whiner. I had so many mixed emotions. I grew up living well, very comfortable. Although we were a dysfunctional family, I still never wanted for anything. I had pretty much whatever my little heart desired. How could either of my parents allow themselves to be so comfortable not knowing if their other offspring had sufficient food or shelter?

"Good morning." Matthew peeked at me under the covers.

"Good morning." It sure was nice having him around. Mom and Aunt Libby thought he was a great catch and warned me not to mess things up with my bratty opinionated attitude. I prayed I wouldn't mess things up. I didn't have a great track record with relationships.

Chapter Fifteen

I couldn't eat on the flight. My stomach was queasy. I had butterflies, no, I think they were dragonflies in my stomach. The plan was for Mr. Benson to meet Jerome at his office first. He was going to hand Jerome a picture of me and answer any pressing questions he had before we met. I'd been to the bathroom four times since we arrived at Ronald Reagan airport. I go a lot when I'm nervous.

I sat in a beautiful courtyard behind the building where Jerome worked, waiting to meet him at any moment. *I'm going to be a big girl, I'm not going to cry, I'm not going to babble, I'm going to give him a chance to ask all the questions. God, I hope he's not a jerk. What if he's a total butt hole towards me? I'm not ready for this. He is a descendant from Dad and Grandpa Adams. That* was probably one of the meanest men I'd ever met in my life and his blood was running through both of my brothers.

A deep voice broke my silent thoughts, "Hello."

I turned around and there stood a gorgeous man. I couldn't speak. I just stared at him as he stepped closer to me. I felt tears rolling down my cheeks. *Oh no. I'm not supposed to cry.* He smiled; I believe it was the warmest smile I'd ever seen. I stood up. He stepped closer and wrapped his arms around me and held me for seconds...minutes I didn't know. He jokingly said, "I'm supposed to be the only one shaking out here." I cleared my throat hoping it would give me the courage to speak. He pushed me back and looked dead into my eyes. "Brittney, my beautiful sister, Brittney. We have a lot to talk about." He giggled. "You're going to have to stop crying and talk to me."

Finally I laughed. "I'm sorry. I'm just so happy to finally meet and see you." I came alive and gave my little brother a big hug. As we sat, I spotted Mr. Benson watching from a nearby water fountain. I waved. He responded with a salute and faded away.

"Before we get too involved, I need to confirm something with you." His kindness grew stern and rigid in a matter of seconds. "Mr. Benson said you didn't have a problem taking a DNA test. Just to play it safe for the both of us. Neither of us wants to get attached about new family members only to find out later is was all just one big misunderstanding."

"Of course, I definitely want to get tested. Before we go any further there's something else I need to share with you."

I had asked Mr. Benson not to tell Jerome about Jaden. I wanted tell him.

"Oh boy, I'm not sure how many other surprises I can handle." Jerome rubbed his hands together and shrugged his shoulders. "Lay it on me."

I took a deep breath and reached into my oversized purse, pulling out the envelope. Jerome watched the envelope as if it were the results from a paternity test on *The Maury Povich Show*. I took out the mug shot of Jaden and gave it to him. He squinted and his breathing became rapid. I thought he was going to hyperventilate. I placed my hand on his shoulder. "That's your twin brother, Jaden. If this is a misunderstanding and I'm not your sister and my mom and dad are not your mom and dad, I think we can both agree this is your brother." He took a deep breath and fought hard to hold back the tears as water filled his eyes.

"He didn't tell me about him. I asked him if there was anything else I should know?" Jerome finally began to breathe normal again. "Before we go any further, are there any other siblings I need to know about?"

I threw my hands up. "Not that I know about. Just us." I took his hand in mine. "I know you have a zillion questions. I'll tell you as much as I know. I also brought pictures of you and Jaden when you were small children." I began digging into my purse for the few pictures I'd taken from mom's little box.

"What do you mean when we were children? We lived together?"

"No. I mean…you were children, but in separate places. Here." I handed him one picture at a time of him when he was a baby, then a few more of him as a young boy. All were with different families and different surroundings. His eyes became cold, his demeanor hardened.

"I remember these days." Jerome chuckled sarcastically. He dropped his head. "These people used to beat the hell out of me every day." He shook his head, staring at the picture again. "Aren't you full of surprises, both sweet and sour."

"I'm sorry. My mom had these pictures. She finally told me who you and Jaden were and why she had them hidden. Here are some of Jaden. She didn't have as many of him."

"Why?"

"Not sure. I think because he was with a stable family." Jerome couldn't hide his anger. I wasn't sure at this point to whom it was directed.

"So now the big question I'm sure you suspect I've been dying to know. Why did she or they give us away?"

As much as I had come to hate my father, I still felt this insane desire to protect his image from his sons. But I knew the truth would come out sooner or later. It always did. I attempted to sugarcoat the truth. "First, let me explain the racism and abuse our parents faced daily."

"Wait." Jerome held up his hand. "What are we mixed with?" Jerome noticed my shocked look, like "you didn't know?" "I was told I was mixed with white, but I was also told I was mixed with Hispanic. Seeing you, though, I think more white."

"You have to excuse me, Jerome. I don't mean to be critical of you, but I would have thought you would have done some digging for yourself to see who you belonged to or where you came from. Didn't you need your birth certificate several times throughout your life?" I caught myself scolding and eased up.

"Yes, I saw my birth certificate, but it stated, 'father unknown.' I was told my mother had died. I guess I could have played detective when I grew up, but I was finally who I wanted to be and where I wanted to be for the first time in my life. You probably couldn't even imagine the kind of life I had. The last thing I wanted to do is go back in time and revisit the horrors I'd managed to escape. To answer your question, no I didn't try to acquire information about my parents. I didn't care if I was black and white, or black and Hispanic, I was just happy to be counted and treated like a human being."

He was right. I couldn't begin to imagine what he'd gone through. What his life had been like being tossed from home to home like a rag doll. "You're right. I don't have a clue, but I'm going to do whatever I can to fill in the blanks and help as much as I can."

"Back to my original question, why did they give us away?"

I had to be extremely careful how I answered this question. "Like I said before, the times were different when they were dating. Our parents came from the south, Selma, Alabama, to be exact. Back then it was very dangerous for interracial couples. Dad was beaten several times and…"

"I wasn't born in Alabama."

"No. We were all born in California."

"I'm sorry to cut you off, but what does racism in Alabama have to do with why they gave us away?"

"I was just trying to give you some background on who they are and what they'd gone through. Although it wasn't as bad in California, they still experienced racial tensions for being together. I'm sure you've seen and heard stories of racial riots in the seventies. There was racial tension everywhere and interracial couples suffered from both sides. Their own families sometimes denied them and the…"

"Brittney, I really don't need you to give me a Black History lesson. If you know why, give it to me straight."

"Your grandfather, our grandfather, convinced Dad he couldn't raise black boys in this society." As much as I tried, there was no way to make this sound okay, reasonable, or logical.

"So what you're telling me is my parents gave me and my brother away because we were black?"

"There's so much more to it than that. We're really simplifying the whole situation with that statement." Jerome peeked at his watch for the second time.

"Are you late for something?" I tried to hide my annoyance.

"Actually, we both have an appointment. I have a good friend that works at the crime lab. He's expecting us at five thirty. He's going to perform our DNA test. I figured after we finished up with him we could get some dinner while we continued catching up on things."

"Ok."

"To be quite honest with you, I'm not sure how much more I want to learn about my parents. It's hard to believe I have a mother who'd just give her son away because it might be a little difficult to raise two biracial boys. She knew creating a family with a white man would be difficult. What kind of woman is that? I guess the stereotype of a black mothers' strength and endurance is definitely one we can debunk, huh?"

"Wait a minute." I paused because I didn't want to let him know right away how awful our father was, but I wasn't going to let him trash Mom after all she'd been through. "I haven't been completely honest with you."

His head dropped again. He clasped his hands together and peered at me. "What now?"

"Mom was forced to give you two up. The reason I was trying to explain to you how it was back in the early seventies was to prepare you for how and why you and Jaden were given up. Our grandfather, our father's father, was the most racist and hateful man I ever knew. He disowned Dad when he refused to leave Mom. I remember when I was a little girl and we'd go back to Selma to visit Grandma and Granddad, Mom's parents and family, Dad would take me over to see his parents. I could tell I wasn't very welcomed." I laughed. "I remember Grandpa Adams say, 'She'd be all right if she didn't have that nigga juice running through her veins.' Although I was young and didn't understand a lot, I knew he didn't approve of me because my mom was black. Anyway, from what I've gathered from Mom, Grandpa Adams somehow convinced Dad if he had boys, black boys, they'd soon turn on him. Of course, I haven't heard Dad's side of this story. He doesn't know I found out about his deep dark secret." I couldn't believe the story I was telling Jerome. I went on with the version I'd received from Mom. "Dad sort of threatened Mom into giving you two up."

"Sort of? Threatened?"

"Yes. He told her he'd take me away and she'd never see me again if she didn't give up the baby if it was a boy. They didn't know they were having twins until you were both born." While telling this story, I realized I still needed more answers. "There was a lot of civil unrest going on back then so I guess Grandpa did a number on Dad. Mom was scared of losing me, so she didn't fight it. I think she felt responsible for all of Dad's pain. The whites in their hometown almost killed him and he lost his family over their relationship."

Jerome quickly glanced at his watch. "We're going to be late if we don't leave now. You rode with Mr. Benson, right?"

"Yes. We figured you wouldn't mind taking me back to the hotel."

"Good. Let's go. Barry isn't too far from here."

We practically ran to the parking lot so I couldn't continue talking until we got to the car. He opened the door to his maroon Jaguar and made sure I was safely buckled in. While driving, he asked the obvious question, "Why didn't she try to find us when you became of age? I mean you're a grown woman now and have been for a long time. What was the problem then?"

I couldn't really give him a sane answer for that question. I'd asked the same question but never received an appropriate answer. "I think she felt it was too late." We arrived at the lab within ten minutes.

We walked in the huge glass doors. The receptionist recognized Jerome, greeting him with a smile accompanied with a little flirting. *She doesn't know me. I could be his woman. She has a lot of nerve.* I quickly pulled myself together and decided not to trip with her. The lab was sterile and chic, if that made any sense. All of the décor was stainless steel and white. There were only a few chairs in the waiting area with a small table with a couple of magazines sprawled out on the table. The receptionist picked up the phone to announce our arrival via intercom. Seconds later, we were greeted by a middle-aged professional-looking white man dressed in a lab coat over a nice pair of navy blue slacks with a freshly pressed powder blue dress shirt and tie. For a white guy, he was very attractive. His deep, dark eyes with those long thick eyelashes were mesmerizing. He seemed to know it so I played it off as if he were a regular average-looking Joe.

"Hey, Barry." Jerome shook his hand and turned to me. "This is the young lady I was telling you about, Brittney Adams."

"Very nice." He extended his hand. "Pleased to meet you."

What the hell am I, a piece of meat? I swore this man was undressing me with his eyes.

"Let's go on in and get this thing done," Jerome said.

Minutes later, we were in Barry's office with both of our mouths swabbed for our DNA tests. "I'll put a rush on this so we'll have the results in twenty-four hours or less. Is that quick enough for you, buddy?" He said it almost in a sarcastically joking manner.

"That would be great." Jerome answered.

We were in and out of the lab within thirty minutes. Jerome and I strolled back to his car. He escorted me to the passenger side and opened and closed the door for me like a true gentleman. He took his seat on the driver's side. "Do you like seafood?"

"Yes, I love seafood, especially in Maryland."

"Great. I'm going to take you out to Jerry's." I hadn't heard of Jerry's, but I was willing and ready for it.

As we drove to the restaurant, I finished explaining the type of relationship I viewed our parents as having. We walked into the restaurant and waited for about fifteen minutes before we were seated. The aroma tantalized my appetite. This was a good pick.

Jerome had been very quiet while we waited. I wasn't sure if it were because he was too pissed off to speak to me or because he didn't want the people around us to hear our conversation. Finally, we were directed to a high leather cushioned booth. He must have planned this. There's no way we lucked up on this booth. Privacy was definitely not an issue. He must bring his dates here. I really wanted to get to know him better, but he had so many questions, which I understood.

"Why aren't you married? You're good-looking, educated, and you seem like a nice guy."

"I guess I haven't found the right person." He brushed over the question. "Back to my parents. I know you said 'our' father." He giggled. "That sounds a little weird for me. I've never referred to any man as father or dad. I know he doesn't know you've found me and Jaden, but does your mom know you were coming to meet me?"

"No. I didn't want to tell her until I met you first."

143

"Well, that's a relief. I thought, she knew I was here and still didn't come with you to see the son she gave away."

"No. I didn't even tell her I found you and Jaden. She's very fragile when it comes to this whole situation." The waiter interrupted and took our orders. I ordered the crab cakes, baked potato, and a salad. Jerome ordered the Mariner's platter. The waiter disappeared and quickly returned with our drinks.

"You're very protective of her, which is understood. She has been your mother all your life."

I told him the little I'd learned about Jaden. We both grew anxious to find him. The waiter brought our food. I was stifled when Jerome immediately bowed his head and said grace aloud for both of us. I patiently waited for him to finish.

"I'd like to find Jaden first and possibly have both of you meet her at the same time. What do you think about that?"

He sat quietly stirring or, rather, playing with his food before answering. "I suppose that wouldn't be a problem. You have an address for him?"

"Mr. Benson said he could get his last known address from his probation officer but wanted to check it out first. He should have something for me by the time I get back." I studied Jerome's every move. "Are you sure it's fine if you meet your brother first and then meet Mom together?"

"Yeah, this will give me some much needed time to process all of this anyway. Yeah, I can definitely wait."

I had a feeling Jerome wasn't too keen on meeting the rest of the family. This was a lot for him to digest.

The next morning, Barry called Jerome to inform him we could come in for the results around two o'clock. Jerome had taken off Friday so we'd met for a late breakfast to try to get to know each other more. We arrived at the lab just before two but had to wait around for about twenty minutes before we were escorted to Barry's office. It wasn't quite an office. It was more like a private lab area where specimens were retrieved and reviewed. There was a long file cabinet and a clear counter for paperwork. Only one chair was available, so we all stood.

"I have good news and bad news." I felt my blood beginning to boil. What kind of bad news could he have? I knew this man was my brother. This was the man in those pictures. I was as sure of that as I was of my own name. Could my mother have lied? Did she have an affair and he was my half brother? I thought I'd pass out until I realized Barry had a ridiculous smirk on his face.

"Relax, Brittney, the bad news is for your brother." He turned to Jerome. "Sorry, dude, this fine woman is your full-blooded sister, so there's no way you can ever date her. Congratulations, you two, you have the same mother and father."

"You're absolutely sure?" Jerome asked.

"Hmmmm, only ninety-nine point nine-nine-nine percent sure." He laughed. "Yes, I'm sure, man. Go take your sister out and celebrate."

We looked at each other like we were scared to touch one another. As if we'd just met all over again. "I already knew it, so I'm good." We embraced. "We have to find Jaden. He looks like he could use us." I said.

"Let's not rush things. Remember he had a family. We don't know what he's been told." We spent most of the rest of the day getting to know each other in the present versus discussing the past to death. I welcomed the change. After he received the confirmation, he seemed much more relaxed with me. He picked me up early Saturday morning and dropped me off at the airport. We said our good-byes and promised to call daily with updates on Jaden. I could breathe. I'd met one of my brothers and he was great.

Chapter Sixteen

I'd left my car at the airport so I didn't have to stand around waiting for anyone to pick me up. Besides, I had a busy day ahead of me. Ms. Wilma called yesterday to tell me Angela wanted to leave; she wanted to find another home. I really needed to get her some outside help, but it wouldn't do any good if she wasn't willing to accept it. Thank goodness I only brought a carry-on so I didn't have to wait for luggage either. I was at my car and driving out of the garage within thirty minutes from the time the plane landed. That had to be a record.

I called Matthew to let him know I'd made it home safely. It was nice having someone to be concerned about me. Then I called Mom to check in with her. She sounded in good spirits. Instead of heading home, I went straight to Ebony Eyes.

The house was empty. That was weird for the middle of a Saturday afternoon. I continued to walk into the dimly lit living room then the kitchen. The heavy black-out curtains were all drawn. Only peeks of light slipped through the windows. An eerie silence possessed the house. I called out several times, but no one answered. Fear quickly consumed me. I called out louder while racing through every room on the first level. Before running upstairs, I checked the schedule for weekend activities, although the schedule for the activities was already sketched in my brain as it was every weekend. I sprinted up the stairs, barging through each door searching to see if anything was out of the ordinary. Minutes into my frantic search, I pulled out my cell phone and began calling Ms. Wilma. Just as she answered, I opened the door to Angela's room. It looked as if a hurricane had swept through her room only. The large five drawer chest had been knocked over, papers were everywhere, and the long mirror on her closet door was cracked.

"Hello? Ms. Brittney?" I snapped back in time to hear an anxious Ms. Wilma on the other end of the phone. "Ms. Brittney, can you hear me now?"

"Yes. Wilma. What in the world happened here? I'm in Angela's room."

"That man came back last night. She had bad nightmares all night. Ms. Cooper told me I should attempt to get her talking about what the man wanted. I told her I knew it wasn't her fault she was pregnant and then Ms. Brittney, she went completely off. She started rantin' and ravin' about how I was all in her business and didn't know jack about her. I tried to calm her down, but she wouldn't listen. She yelled for me to get out of her room. I left but I heard bashing and thumping noises, so I ran back upstairs to make sure she was all right. She'd knocked the chest over and trashed the room. Then she bent over holding her stomach and began yelling in pain. I brought her to the hospital. We're here at Kaiser now. You know that new girl, Tracie, already called in sick so I had to bring all the girls with me."

"Ok, Ms. Wilma, I'll be right there to relieve you. You did the right thing to take her to the hospital. Has she been seen by the doctor?"

"No, not yet, but I think she's next."

"Good. I'm on my way."

"Thank you. You know my girls are getting restless."

"Dammit." I didn't have the heart to scold Wilma over the phone for opening her mouth about Angela's pregnancy, but I had instructed Ms. Cooper to tell the staff not to mention any knowledge of her situation to her. No one was supposed to know about the rape because Angela didn't see it that way. I was sure Ms. Cooper reminded the staff of this – she was totally reliable. Ms. Wilma probably forgot in the midst of her panic. What a way to knock me off that natural high I experienced a while ago. Thank goodness she was still under her mother's Kaiser plan so we wouldn't have to go to the county.

Most of our girls' parents had decent insurance except for one, Sandra, and she used to be in constant need of some kind of medical attention. She'd been quiet lately.

Maybe the thought of motherhood was finally kicking in. I couldn't believe Ms. Wilma was at the hospital with all five girls. She was tough, though. Thank goodness Dinora wasn't scheduled to work. No doubt she would have made the situation much worse. Then again, at least Dinora came to work when she was scheduled. This new chick had to go. Weekends were usually the drama days and the last thing we needed were sick calls on the weekend.

About fifteen minutes later, I swerved into the patient parking lot off Edgemont. I darted right past the little security guard by the pharmacy. I didn't know why they had him there. He just occupied valuable space. I made it to the emergency area and immediately began scanning the room for the girls. I spotted Wilma and the rest of the crew. The other patients probably thought there was a Lamaze class for teens by watching the four young pregnant girls. You would have thought they'd been there all night the way each of them whined.

"Ms Brittney, I'm glad to see you."

"Where's Angela?"

"She's still in there." Ms. Wilma pointed towards the wide double doors.

"They said the doctor will see her in about five more minutes, but they said that ten minutes ago, so who knows?"

Ms. Wilma told me Angela was in the third room on the right, behind the doors. I walked in and found Angela curled up in a ball. "Hi, Angela."

"I don't want to talk to you. Please leave," she mumbled.

150

"I know you're upset and I don't want to upset you more, but we're going to have to talk sooner or later. I'd rather we talk first before you have to talk to a social worker or the police."

She grinned wickedly. "I don't believe you. You have the nerve to come in here and threaten me about telling the police? It's my word against yours, lady."

"Angela, I should have called the police already. I'm not an official mandated reporter, but I am obligated by the state to report any suspected abuse. Rape is included in that. The only reason I haven't reported this to the police is because both of you were drunk and you still consider this guy your friend. So what's it going to be, Angela?"

Before she could answer, the doctor came in to examine her. I left the room to give them privacy for the physical examination. The doctor stepped out. He told me and the nurse he was ordering an Ultrasound. He asked the nurse to call him when it was done. I stepped back into the room with Angela, still treading carefully to not upset her.

"I'll talk to you, but not now. You don't need to call anyone. Like you said, we were drunk and had sex and that's how I got pregnant. Let's drop it. I just want to go home." She sounded hopeless. Her last words to me were "go home." I wondered which home she was speaking of.

Ms. Wilma took the other girls home while I waited for Angela. I called Matthew to update him and to let him know I'd be late.

The doctor ordered complete bed rest for Angela for the next couple of days. She had a small amount of bleeding so he asked her to return next week. If everything was okay, she'd resume her regular appointments. I took her straight home. We didn't speak the entire drive home. When we arrived, the girls were getting ready for the movies. *Oh no, I'm going to have to stay here until they return.* Angela made a beeline for her room and slammed the door. I didn't have the heart to tell Ms. Wilma to cancel their outing, so I dragged myself to the office and called to check on Mom. I decided to hold off on canceling my evening with Matthew. I really wanted to see him even if I fell out from exhaustion into his arms. It'd be worth it.

"Hey, Mom, How are you?"

"Hi, Princess. Everything is fine. Are you back in town?"

"Yes. Is Aunt Libby still there?"

"No. She left yesterday. Remember, she was meeting friends in Hawaii. She told me to tell you to call her as soon as you get a chance."

"I'll call her next week."

"Are you coming over tonight? I miss you. I want to see my little Princess."

"I miss you, too, Mom, but unfortunately there was an incident here at the home and one of the girls had to go to the hospital."

"Who?"

"Angela."

"Is she all right?"

"Yes, but wouldn't you know it? The new girl called in sick already so I need to stay here with Angela because Ms. Wilma took the other girls to the movies."

"You're going to work yourself into an early grave if you don't slow down, young lady. How was your business in… where did you go again?"

"Maryland, Mom, and it went fine. I need to talk to you later. I have to go now, okay?"

"Okay, sweetie. Talk to you soon."

I knew I needed to avoid Mom until I got myself together.

"Hey, you." I looked up. Ms. Cooper stood at the door gleaming at me.

"Ms. Cooper? What are you doing here?" Ms. Cooper walked in, plopping in the seat across from my desk. She was a well-kept, tall, physically fit woman with a mental strength to match. A fifty-six year young woman who'd dedicated her time to Ebony Eyes Home for the five years it had been open. She was so passionate about helping and caring for the girls, I was surprised she hadn't opened up a home herself.

"Ms. Wilma called me after they came from the hospital. I didn't tell her I was coming because I wanted to make sure my sister would keep my grandchildren for a few hours. I know you just got back today. You shouldn't have to come and work here, too. Have you been home yet?"

"You're so wonderful. I wish I could clone you." I smiled. "No, I haven't been home yet. I really appreciate you coming in this evening. I'm going to grab my stuff and get out of here." I gave Ms. Cooper a big hug and kiss and practically ran out the door.

I checked my messages as soon as I got home. I was surprised to hear Mr. Benson's voice. He usually called me on my cell.

"Hello, Brittney. I decided to leave this message on your home number because I didn't want to interrupt your time with your brother. I have a last-known address for Jaden, but I am going to check it out first. I want to talk to him face to face before you two meet. I hope you and Jerome had a good visit. One down and one to go. I'll talk to you tomorrow."

I hoped Mr. Benson would find Jaden soon. I wasn't sure how much longer I could hold off telling Mom I'd found her sons. I didn't know how she would handle this information or what she'd do with it, but her sons had a right to meet their biological mother – at least if they wanted to. My mind went back to Jaden's parents. What type of parents were they? Were they supportive? Were they abusive? Sometimes parents did all the right things and their children somehow went astray. Maybe he had too much of Dad in him? On the other hand, Jerome never remained in one home for more than three or four years and he turned out to be a successful attorney. Who would've thought?

The phone woke me up bright and early at eight sharp. Normally I was up by now, but Matthew and I stayed up all night talking about my trip to Prince George's County. Although I had a pretty rough homecoming when Matthew came over and I began telling him about the trip, the adrenaline rushed through my body all over again. The jet lag disappeared and we talked all night. I believe I repeated every word of all the conversations I had with Jerome. I was like a schoolgirl telling her mom about her prom night or first date.

"Hello?"

"I hope I didn't wake you, Brittney, but I have news about Jaden." I jumped up. I turned around to poke Matthew, but he wasn't there.

"What is it? Did you see him last night? Does he know I'm looking for him? Does he know...?"

"Brittney, please calm down." He chuckled. "I'm sorry if I made you feel there was more news than what I have to deliver today. I checked out the address and asked the neighbors if he lived there. Most of them wouldn't talk to me even after I swore he wasn't in any trouble, but one woman told me he did live there and was one of the nice ones. I do have to say, he does not live in a very safe-looking area. I would like to reiterate that I need to find him first. This is why I don't feel comfortable giving you any more information on him."

I told Mr. Benson I understood. Although, I wanted to tell him I was a big girl and could handle it. I jumped out of bed and ran into the kitchen where I found Matthew frying bacon and eggs. I shared the information I'd received and went back to wash up for breakfast. I wondered, *What kind of life is Jaden living?*

Chapter Seventeen

"I'm walking out of this door in ten minutes so you better be ready," Richard said.

"I'm ready. I just have to put on my lipstick and..."

"I don't know what you keep trying to paint your face for. All that stuff makes you look stupid. You must think somebody's trying to check you out. You must have forgotten how old you are. Nobody's checking you out."

Marilyn stood in front of the mirror leaning over the dresser digging in an oversized Mahogany jewelry box searching desperately to find the perfect earrings for the outfit she was wearing. "No Richard, I know no one is 'checking me out,' but I'd still like to look nice for my husband. Aren't you happy I try to keep myself together? I thought all men liked that." She said as she found the earrings and was placing one in her ear.

By the time those words came out of her mouth, Richard had snatched her by the arm, twisted her around to face him and was yelling, "You don't need to worry about what all men like. Do you hear me! You only need to worry about what I like and what I say. Every time I look around, you're worrying about what somebody else is thinking or saying. You better get it in your thick skull I'm the only one you need to be thinking about when it comes to what anyone thinks." He shook her forcibly back and forth holding her inches from his face. "Do you understand me?" Marilyn's eyes widened with terror. "Do you hear me?" He shouted again while still shaking her ferociously.

Marilyn shook her head yes while her entire body quivered in fear. Richard pushed her back into the dresser and walked out of the room. Marilyn turned around and watched herself in the mirror, still shaking. Tears sprang into her eyes. She took in a deep breath, picked up her pace, and began patting her face dry in a panic. She only had about five minutes to get it together or he'd be back. She felt a stinging sensation on her ear. She pulled her hair back and noticed blood on her earlobe. She studied closer and realized the earring she'd just placed in her ear before Richard grabbed her, had scraped her earlobe and there was a deep scratch. She sprinted into the bathroom grabbed a cotton swab and doused it with hydrogen peroxide, wiping her ear and hurrying to the garage to get into the car to meet the time limit, ten minutes.

Church was only twenty minutes away. Apparently Richard decided to exhibit his excellent time-management skills by using this time to reprimand Marilyn by explaining how awful of a wife she was and had been. "I don't know why you always do things to provoke me when I'm trying to get in the right attitude to go to serve God. I'm trying to go and worship the Lord and you have to mess that up. You never know when to just keep your big mouth closed, do you?" Marilyn sat quietly looking like a deflated weather-beaten tire. "I'm the one that takes care of you, buying you almost everything you want. Sometimes you act like you have amnesia, like you don't know all I do for you. You've got people thinking you're not happy with me. Do you think your life is miserable?" Richard paused for an answer. "That wasn't a rhetorical question, Marilyn, answer me." He yelled.

Marilyn finally responded. "No, Richard."

"I don't get you. After all I've done for you and after all I've given up for you, you're never satisfied." Richard slammed his hand on the dashboard then pointed his index finger in Marilyn's face. "I'm getting real sick of this mess!"

Richard veered off the busy street into the parking lot of the church they'd attended for the past fifteen years. Still chastising Marilyn, Richard swerved into an open space, almost hitting Sister Jackson as she strutted from the front of a blue Honda Accord. Richard slammed on the brakes. Marilyn and Sister Jackson simultaneously clutched their chest. Richard waved to Sister Jackson to continue, but she threw her hand up in retreat and dotted to the left to avoid the space all together. "Richard, you have to slow down in the parking lot." Marilyn looked at Richard's deadly eyes and quickly tried to soften her comment. "There are so many people walking around here…"

"Shut up. Now you're gonna tell me how to drive? What? Now you think I'm stupid, too."

The pastor's sermon was on Christian relationships, based on Ephesians 5:25. Husbands, love your wives, even as Christ also loved the church and gave himself for it. Pastor Jones paced back and forth in the pulpit shouting to the congregation of God's love for the church comparing and using that love as an example of the type of love a husband should possess for his wife. Richard nodded his head in agreement of everything that was said as he sat on the royal blue pew in the second row of the large church. When the pastor finished and raised his hands for the congregation to stand, Richard jumped up clapping and shouting repeatedly, "Amen, Amen."

Marilyn stood next to him like a Stepford wife. Poised and perfectly dressed, she began to join in on the clapping and said, "Amen," quietly not to outshine her husband.

As the churchgoers exited the building, they shook hands with Pastor Jones. Marilyn and Richard made small steps toward the minister as if they were marching to the Jordan River to be baptized by John the Baptist. Finally reaching Pastor Jones, he took Marilyn's hand. "Hello, Brother and Sister Adams, how are you two doing?" Before Marilyn could answer, Richard put his hand around her waist and squeezed her side.

"Everything is great, Pastor Jones. How's Sister Jones?" Marilyn answered softly with a rehearsed planted smile.

"She's good. Now tell me this," he still held Marilyn's hand, "is your husband here..." he pointed to Richard, "loving you the way he should?" He laughed.

"Oh, yes. I have no complaints." Marilyn spruced up to convince the pastor of her façade.

"All right. That's good to hear. You keep taking good care of this sweet lady. You hear me?"

"Yes, Pastor, I'll do my best." Richard smiled.

Richard rushed past everyone by saying quick hellos while casting a forged smile to all that dared to get in his way.

The car ride home was long and quiet. Marilyn was nervous as usual. She never knew what would trigger her husband's rage. It could be something as small and innocent as a half smile from a man or a conversation that continued seconds too long with other women. One time Richard went completely off on Marilyn because she was laughing too much with Brittney. He'd accused Marilyn of siding with their daughter and mocking him. She wondered why her husband was so insecure and paranoid. He was a lieutenant. He was respected by all and feared by most, but at home, he was a paranoid little boy constantly trying to prove himself.

Marilyn dashed into their room and changed her clothes immediately. She hurried to the kitchen to begin cooking as she did every Sunday afternoon. She scooted around grabbing pots and pans from the cabinets. She grabbed fresh broccoli and carrots from the refrigerator and a small cutting board from beneath the sink and started cutting and washing the vegetables.

Marilyn's back was turned to the door. Marilyn reached towards a cabinet when she caught a glimpse of Richard standing idle at the doorway watching her, which startled her. "Did you need something?"

"Did I say I needed something?" Richard growled as he walked to the cabinet to get a glass and then to the fridge. He placed the glass in the cove outside of the refrigerator and pushed to receive water. Richard stared motionless at the water filling the glass. He gulped the water down and placed the glass in the sink and stood next to Marilyn. "So were you lying to Pastor Jones?"

She was puzzled. "Lying about what?"

"About me loving you the way you should be loved and not having any complaints."

Marilyn took in a breath. "Yes, I was lying." Marilyn looked as shocked in her response as Richard did but continued expressing her feelings. "Sometimes you treat me like a queen like you did when we first met and then sometimes you treat me like you hate me. You act like you can't stand the sight of me. I'm not sure why we're still together. We both have lost a lot and caused each other a tremendous amount of heartache and pain, but we keep holding on to each other. Why?"

"You're a real piece of work. Sometimes I wonder are you just blind, stupid, or both? I'm the only one that has lost anything from this relationship. I'm the one that lost the respect and love from my parents. You still have your parents. My parents died hating me because of you. My own brother and sister, to this day, won't speak to me – my own flesh and blood. My aunts and uncles, cousins, nieces, and nephews, all of my family will have nothing to do with me and you say we both have lost. There's no comparison!" Richard screamed, pointing his finger in her face.

A stream of tears covered Marilyn's face. She finally gazed directly into his eyes. "You're standing here telling me about losing flesh and blood. Have you forgotten what I lost because of you? How dare you stand here complaining and comparing relationships and people lost due to this so-called marriage." Her grip on the knife she held became tighter and tighter as her anger grew. She suddenly felt pain in her hand. Looking down, she realized her nails were piercing her palm. She turned back to Richard and pointed the knife in his face, "Don't you ever talk to me about what you've lost because of me!" She threw the knife into the sink and walked out heading down the long narrowed hallway to the bedroom.

Richard followed closely behind her. "Who in the hell do you think you're talking to like that?" That was his favorite line. She ignored him and went into the closet and grabbed her sneakers. "Where do you think you're going?"

"I need some air. I'm going for a drive." She sat on the bed bent over tying her shoes. Then for the first time in a long time she stood tall, feeling the full length of her five foot seven slim body. "I'm going out." As soon as the words came out of her mouth, she felt an immediate burning sensation to her face. Richard slapped her, knocking her back down to the bed. Pouncing on her like a tiger attacking his prey, he palmed her chin and jawbone with one hand, confining her to the bed.

"You're not going anywhere unless I say you're going. You got that? Don't get so high and mighty that you get yourself hurt. Now, I'll tell you what you're going to do. You're going to get up and get your butt back in the kitchen and finish cooking dinner. Do you understand?" Marilyn didn't answer. Richard squeezed her jaw tighter and gritted his teeth. "I said, do you understand?" Again, Marilyn didn't answer. Her fear subsided. Her anger and hatred for her husband took over her body. She kneed him and pushed him off of her and ran, but Richard caught her in the hallway and threw her against the wall. "What the hell has gotten into you today?" He seemed baffled and enraged by her actions. He turned her face and knees towards the wall. He held her hands behind her back like he'd done so many times in the past, when he was a beat cop, with the thugs on the street just before placing the handcuffs on them. He probably wasn't taking another chance on getting kicked. He leaned in, resting his chin on her shoulder with his cheek pressed against hers and whispered, "You owe me."

"I don't owe you anymore. I'm tired of paying for your family's racist attitude. I don't owe you. I paid that debt over thirty years ago. I don't owe you anymore." She sobbed.

Richard released her. "Do what you want to do." He walked into the family room and sat in his, I'm the King, oversized La-Z-Boy chair.

Marilyn slid down to the floor right where he left her in the hallway and buried her head into her hands, weeping. She watched the front door, as if she needed it to persuade her to walk out of it. Minutes later, she got up from the

163

floor, went into the bathroom, washed her face, and untied her shoes, placing them back into the closet. Everything was just as she'd left it in the kitchen. She finished cooking and prepared a plate for her husband and took it to him, placing it on a tray in front of him. She immediately vanished from his sight and retired into the guest room and closed the door behind her.

After minutes of lying on the bed, Marilyn went to the closet, dug through the barriers, and retrieved the pictures of her sons. She took one picture of each of them out and went back to the bed. She traced their faces with her fingers. She lay on the bed reminiscing of that horrible day when her sons were taken from her, never getting a chance to hold them or look at their beautiful innocent faces.

Marilyn recalled again how Richard had tricked her into signing the release forms for the adoption. He'd asked her to sign a bunch of paperwork for the insurance and hospital stay. Richard had added the adoption papers into the pile and she just signed where he pointed without reading any of the headings on any of the papers. Richard had also spoken privately to the doctor, nurses, and social worker without Marilyn's knowledge.

Ever since she'd confessed to Brittney how she lost her sons, the memories kept replaying over and over again in her mind almost daily.

It was hard to keep her weight up because she was so stressed out worrying if she was carrying a boy or a girl. Back then, the older women told you if you were having a boy or girl based on how low you carried the baby. Everyone around her mentioned she was having a boy because her belly was low. She prayed all day every day God would bless her with a girl so she wouldn't have to give her child up. She prayed if the child was a boy it would be whiter looking so she'd have a chance of keeping her son.

She stared at the dingy white popcorn ceiling, grinned, shaking her head while tears welled in her eyes. "For two days I sat in that hospital pretending to be polite, cooperative, and patient so I could see my beautiful Princess once again. I vowed to get my sons back after I could insure Brittney's and my safety. That day never came. Instead I cowered to Richard and all his demands. I've lived in fear for so long it became as normal to me as eating and sleeping. Brittney's right. I've had plenty of opportunities to leave and didn't. I can't blame my condition – my misery – on Richard anymore. This is all my doing now."

Chapter Eighteen

Matthew and I rushed to the home after receiving a call from Ms. Cooper. Matthew followed me. Thank goodness there was no Sunday morning traffic. Two of the ladies had gotten into a scuffle again. I didn't know if they'd ever learn to handle their differences in a more mature way. When we arrived, Cherokee bombarded us with explanations as soon as we stepped foot inside the door. Seconds later, there came Maria with her story. Cherokee had a long scratch across her face.

"I'm sick of her walking around here like she's all that. She keeps getting in my face. She's just jealous of me 'cause my boyfriend cares about me and always comes to see me and hers don't give a ..." As upset as Cherokee was, she knew the most important rules of the house were no profanity and no fighting. I gave her a hard stare before she continued with what I knew would escape her mouth. She paused. "Crap about her. That's why she's jealous. I'm sick of her hatin' on me. She needs to go because I was here first."

"Calm down, Cherokee. I want you to go with Ms. Dinora so she can tend to that scratch. Are you hurt anywhere else?"

"No, but are you going to kick her out because she's just been causing trouble since she got here?"

"I'm going to have a talk with Maria now. You go get taken care of." Cherokee turned around and sucked her teeth like a spoiled child that had just been told no in a toy store.

Matthew stood inside the foyer, frowning with disgust at the girls.

"I'm going to be over here." he pointed towards the living room. "I know you got this covered." He chuckled and winked at me as he trotted over to the couch, grabbed the remote, and flopped down.

Thanks a lot. I could use a manly presence, but then again I never want the girls to think we can't handle them. Don't want to set a precedent we will not and cannot keep. As much as I wanted to ignore Cherokee's demand to remove Maria from the home, she was right. Ever since Maria moved into Ebony Eyes, there were problems in the house and an unusual amount of tension. "Maria, we need to talk in my office. Let's go."

She traipsed in behind me. We spoke for over an hour. She had an excuse for every single thing I brought up where she was involved with an altercation or incident in the home since her arrival. I tried to wind down the conversation because I knew Matthew was probably getting antsy by now. Maria had already stood up to leave when Matthew poked his head in the door. "Excuse me, but I need to see you right away."

I jumped up and practically threw the shuffling Maria out of the office. "What's going on?" I gestured for him to sit but then realized he'd become a little eager.

"We need to go now. Angela just darted out of here."

"Let's go." I grabbed my keys from my messy desk and ran out. I yelled, "I'm gone, Ms. Cooper. I'll call you later."

By the time we got out of the house and to the driveway, Angela was down the street. We didn't want to draw any attention to ourselves, so we jumped in his car and sat there until we saw her gentleman friend get into his car. Angela began walking back towards the house. We pulled out and drove in the opposite direction. We rode down the next street over, hoping we'd catch up with him on the main artery of the area. We did. This time we were determined to go all the way. Wherever or whenever he stopped, we'd finally speak to him. We followed him to the same neighborhood as the last time, down Sunset to Vermont. We made a right on Vermont and traveled south before making another right turn onto the same street with several apartment buildings. We watched the man from a distance get out of the car and go into one of the dreary looking buildings. We parked down a ways and ran to the building he'd just entered.

"Don't go in here like you're the new sheriff in town," Matthew reminded me. "We don't know what we're walking into."

"Okay, okay, but hurry before we lose him." We walked up to a large wrought iron gate, which made it look like it might be a secured building, but the gate wasn't locked. Matthew pulled open the huge, squeaky gate, and we entered into a dark walkway reeking of urine. It looked as if night had suddenly fallen on us as soon as we entered the dark corridor. We took a few steps in and heard voices coming from the courtyard. We hurried towards the voices, but none of the three men standing had the physique of the man we followed. Although we didn't get a good look at his face, we knew he was at least six feet tall and wore a hooded sweatshirt. The men before us were all under five nine for sure. They appeared to be OGs or whatever you called old gang members from back in the day still trying to hold on to whatever street rep they might have possessed in their younger years. The building appeared to be a haven for drug addicts. There was some light in the courtyard from the sunlight outside due to the opening at the top, but there were dark tunnels leading to different areas of the complex.

"Excuse me?" I displayed absolutely no fear. "Did you see the guy that just walked in here?"

"Who wants to know?"

"Me." I said.

Matthew quickly covered for my naiveté response. "Ummm, we just saw an old friend of ours walk in here. We were trying to catch up with him, but we didn't see which way he went. Did you see him?"

"Yeah, he went that way." A man appearing to be of Latino and Black heritage pointed towards the darkest of the three tunnels.

"Thanks." Matthew grabbed me quickly before I could say another word.

We dashed through the tunnel, looking around at all the doors as if we were searching for a specific apartment number. We'd almost walked the length of the entire hallway, knowing we'd lost him again, yet refusing to give up. The tunnel was cold and desolate. Each step reminded me of being in a cold, hard dungeon. The only things missing were shackles on my feet and chains hanging from the walls. As we approached the end of the tunnel, we heard a sound, a brush against the wall. We both looked back at the same time and then gazed at each other. I think at that very moment we were both thinking the same thing, "We better get the hell out of here." As soon as we turned around to complete our search, Matthew was hit from the back. He staggered towards the cracked cement but swiftly reclaimed his balance before hitting the ground. He stood, instantly pulling me behind him. We looked up, glaring straight into the barrel of one of those nine or ten millimeter all black Beretta guns. Holding it was the man that had pointed us in this direction. Matthew held up both hands in front of him, showing he was willing to cooperate, I guessed. I've never quite understood why people immediately put their hands up before being given any instructions to do so.

"What the hell do you really want and why are you snooping around here?"

At that point, I didn't know what to say. Should I tell the truth? Stick with the lie Matthew had already told? Or shut up and let Matthew do the talking? I decided on the latter. Matthew stood convincingly. "Look, man, we don't want any trouble. I told you, we saw an old friend and just wanted to say hi, that's all."

"You must take me for a fool. What's your old friend's name?"

Matthew swallowed deep., "Richard. Richard Haskell."

"Well, there's no Richard Haskell living here and this isn't the first time you guys have been nosing around here. I saw you a couple of weeks ago. My friend spotted you following him and we watched you drive around the building. Now I don't know if you've really mistaken him for someone else or not, but if you come around here again, you won't leave the same way you came. Got it?"

I could tell Matthew was pissed that this guy punked him in front of me, but I was glad he had sense enough not to try to show his manhood with that big gun staring us in the face. He just obliged him by saying, "Yeah, man." The man stepped aside and waved the gun for us to leave. Matthew shoved me by the waist and we belted out of the drab hall, never once looking back. We made it to the car in about twenty seconds flat.

"Are you okay?" I asked.

Matthew closed his eyes and drew in a long deep breath. When his eyes opened he gave me a cold stare. "Now do you understand why I don't want you following up on this by yourself? We could both have been killed over this mess.

You don't even know if that little brat is telling you the truth about what happened or not."

"I'm sure…"

Matthew held his hand up. "Stop. You're not sure of anything. Just get in the car, please."

I got in the car and pulled the seat belt across my lap and fastened myself in. I knew Matthew didn't want to hear anything I had to say right now, but that didn't stop me from giving my observation and opinion of what had just taken place. "Matthew, this just validates what Angela told me. This is why she's so nervous. These people are dangerous. Maybe she thinks the kid is her friend, but the guy we're looking for is probably threatening her, maybe even her family, if she tells the police."

"Then you should tell the social worker everything so the police can get involved and come around here and officially question these guys."

I'd promised Angela I wouldn't report this to the social worker, but it was my duty. I wanted to talk to the guy first, but I guess I really didn't have a choice any more. "I thought you carried or were licensed to carry a gun?"

"I am." Matthew answered.

"Well, maybe you should have brought it with you."

Matthew eyes met mine with a bone-chilling look. "I do have it with me. Would you have preferred that I try to use it and got us caught up in a gun battle with the two of us versus all of them?" Matthew sounded truly irritated with me.

"We don't know how many of them were there."

He looked at me as if I'd said the most stupidest thing he'd ever heard. "That's exactly my point. We were in their territory. We didn't know what we were walking into." When he stopped at a red light, he turned to me. "Promise me you won't go back there or try to follow this guy again. It's time to let the police handle it. I can press charges against this guy and that will open up an investigation that might get us more information on the guy you're looking for. Think about it." His concern for me protruded through his obvious disappointment and frustration with me.

"I don't want to get you in anymore danger. They might come after you if you press charges."

"This kid was a little street thug. He just wanted to scare us so we wouldn't nose around in his turf."

He dropped me back off at the home. I hopped in my car and jetted to Mom and Dad's. I knew they'd be back from church by now and I'd rather visit now so Matthew and I could have some more quiet time later in the evening.

Visiting Mom had become more of a chore than joy lately. She seemed so somber. Most of my adult life I'd seen my mom acting out a role. A role she began when she said, "I Do." Her entire life had been one scene after another. The mask she wore to hide the pain she was feeling and had felt for a long time was fading. She either didn't have the strength or desire to carry on the charade. The hopelessness I saw in her now came long before she told me about Jerome and Jaden. I wondered if she'd ever spoken to Dad about them. I knew he didn't know she'd kept up with them for as long as she had, but I wondered if Dad ever thought about them? "God, he's such a jerk. I can't believe that man is my father." I decided not to tell Mom about Jerome until we'd found Jaden, but every time I spoke to her or saw her it would be more difficult to keep this secret. Also, I didn't want the only picture I had to show her of Jaden to be a mug shot. The guilt would eat her alive.

The 101 freeway was surprisingly empty. It was a good day for driving. Thinking so much of Jerome and Jaden, I almost missed my exit. I swerved over just in time to get off at Balboa. I was so hungry I decided to drive to Tony Roma's to get their Santa Fe Chicken salad. Mom liked it, too. *I should bring food today just to piss Dad off. Disrupt his Sunday routine.* I veered off Ventura right into the parking lot. It seemed the missing crowd from the freeway was definitely in this parking lot. I finally found a parking space and walked in. I was skeptical to order anything from the overly tattooed young lady standing behind the counter. She was pasty white with midnight black eye shadow and an earring piercing her left eyebrow. She looked like death, skinny and lifeless. Well, at least she had a job. I ordered two Santa Fe Chicken salads to go. I could smell the rolls while I sat on the hard wood chair waiting for my order. Crowds of churchgoers poured in. I hadn't seen this many church dresses with matching fancy purses and shoes in a long time. Too many minutes had passed before the young tattoo lady from behind the counter called me up. "Miss, your order is ready."

"Thank you." I picked up my order and was off to purposely bug my father.

The tree-lined street was beautiful. The trees were blooming with white buds. They appeared like cherry blossoms, but they weren't – definitely a close second. I pulled into the driveway and noticed the open door. *Good they're home.* Of course they would be. I reached for my purse and the two big bags from Tony's. The screen door was unlocked. I walked in. The house was always quiet, but today there was a deadly silence. I peeked in the family room and saw the back of Dad's head. The television was on, but the volume was barely audible. I was curious to know what he was doing. I tiptoed around to see him. He was asleep. He looked as if he'd been there for a while. He looked so sweet, kind, and gentle rammed back in his chair. Next to him was a plate with a half eaten dinner. That was unusual for Dad not to gorge down his entire meal and to have his Sunday meal in the family room verses at the table with Mom. I stood over him, watching him sleep. *Boy did you turn out to be a disappointment.*

I quietly backed out of the room, careful not to wake him, and headed for the kitchen. I placed the bags on the table and darted towards the hall looking for Mom. I called out quietly for her, trying not to wake Dad. Their bedroom door was shut. Gently, I knocked while turning the knob to enter. No Mom. I went further down the hall to the left to one of the guest bedrooms. This door was also shut. I opened the door and peeked in. She lay across the bed. "Mom?" She didn't move or answer. She usually kept her church clothes on while she cooked dinner. She'd put on her slippers and wrap an apron or housecoat over her clothes, but that was different today, too. What was going on here? One thing about my parents, they were both very predictable, especially when it came to Sundays. They were

175

in church every Sunday and came straight home. Dad would sit in his big man-chair while Mom cooked a large meal with dessert. They'd sit down to eat together around three thirty. This was strange. Mom should barely be cleaning the pots and pans now but instead, she was sleeping in the guest room. I hated to wake her, but this was crazy. I shook her, "Mom, wake up." I startled her.

"Hey, Princess," she managed to slur out. "What are you doing here?"

"I came to visit. Why are you in here sleeping? What happened?"

"Nothing happened. I just fell asleep, that's all." She delicately maneuvered her body to an upright position, wiping her slightly red, puffy eyes.

"Have you been crying?"

"No. I just didn't sleep good last night. Enough with the questions. Give me a hug." She wrapped her arms around me. "It's so good to see you."

"I didn't come alone." Her eyes stretched as big as an owl's. She ran her fingers through her hair to smooth it back into place. Always prim and proper.

"Who did you bring with you?"

"Relax, Mom, not who, but what?"

Her small worn face lit up. "What did you bring?"

"Something from Tony Roma's."

She bounced up. "My Santa Fe Chicken salad."

It was so easy to make her happy. "Yeah. Let's go eat or have you eaten?"

"No. I wasn't hungry earlier."

That was strange, too. I decided to leave it alone.

176

When we reached the family room, she turned to go in. I stopped her. "He's asleep."

"Oh, well, let's eat," she whispered.

I rushed to the drawer to get forks. I was beginning to feel weak from hunger.

"Princess." I knew that tone. "Why didn't you bring your father one?"

"Why would I do that? He always acts like he doesn't want anything or doesn't like anything unless you cooked it. Why bother?"

"It's the thought. Don't you think he feels left out when you bring me little treats and you don't include him? He'd never admit it, but that hurts his feelings."

It took all of my being to maintain a respectful tone. "Do you think I give a rat's butt about his feelings right now?" I glared deep into her eyes and handed her a fork. She sat and began eating. We sat at the white tiled table in silence for a few minutes.

"How are you and Matthew doing?"

My tensed body fell flat. I wanted to have a pleasant visit with her without her defending Dad and me not giving her any reason to. The mention of Matthew's name put a smile on my face. "Matthew and I are fine."

"I see. Why don't you have him over for dinner so your father can meet him?"

Damn, she went there again with that father stuff. I wanted to say, "No, why don't I have Jerome over so Dad can meet him?" I didn't. I held my tongue and figured this would be a short visit. Mom seemed to notice the look on my face changed dramatically, but she couldn't take her words back. "Why would you think I'd want Matthew to meet Dad? It's not like he's an ideal father, now is he?"

"No, but he's your father – ideal or not. Regardless of what he or we have done in the past, we're both still your parents. You can't be angry with him only. I was there, too. I didn't do all a mother – a good mother – would have done. You can't just blame him."

"Wow. You're so brainwashed. Mom, you were threatened. You had to choose between them and me."

"He worked hard for us to have a good life. He provided us with everything we needed and most of everything we wanted. He did everything in his power to make up for that." She whispered, looking towards the door to make sure we were still alone.

"Dad used to be a nice man, but later, I guess after he felt he'd made up for his horrible sins, he started treating you like crap. He still does. He talks to you like you're lower than dirt. You're not his wife, you're his slave. You're not even the house nigga. You're his field nigga." As soon as those hateful words slipped from my tongue, I regretted them. This was my mom, the woman who loved me, cared for me, would do anything in the world for me, who gave her sons up for me. "Mom, I'm so sorry. I didn't mean that. I'm so sorry. Please forgive me." I got up, stepped to her, and embraced her, holding her tight.

She gazed up with tears in her eyes. "You're right. I'm nothing to him. He hates me. After all I tried to do to make things better. I even forgave him for the horrible things he made me do and he still…" She buried her head in my arm.

"Mom, let's go, take a drive. Don't wake him up. Just leave him a note. Let's just go. Please." To my surprise, she agreed. She tiptoed to her room, grabbed her sneakers and purse, and returned to the kitchen. I snatched the half-eaten salads and tossed everything into the garbage. Mom sat and quickly jotted a note for Dad, and left it on the table. We snuck out the front door like two thieves in the night.

I hadn't planned this, so I had no clue where we should go, but I was naturally guided towards the 405 freeway heading south. I decided to take the 10 freeway to Santa Monica. It was warm. We could walk on the boardwalk or go to the Promenade. There would be shopping and eateries all around us over there. So, off we went. At least I had a plan now. I felt so guilty. I'd just done the same thing to my Mom I accused my father of doing. Hurting her when all she gave was love to everyone around her. "Mom. I'm really sorry for…"

"Shhh. Forget it. Let's not talk about any of our family issues. Let's just enjoy each other and have a wonderful day." She already looked a hundred times happier than I'd seen her look in a long time. Her demeanor had taken a one hundred and eighty degree turn.

"Sure. Just pure unadulterated fun today. Which would you like to go to first, the Santa Monica Pier or the Promenade?"

"The Pier."

"Then we're off to the Pier." I turned the music up and spotted Mom looking out the window and smiling peacefully.

I pulled into a parking structure where we could walk to both places without moving the car. Mom and I were both walkers. We could go for miles without tiring out. Mom hopped out of the car, sprinting up the busy street like a woman strutting to receive a marathon trophy.

"This is such a beautiful day. I feel like I can breathe for the first time in a long time." She clasped her arm in mine. "Remember when we used to bring you here when you were a little girl? You liked that so much. You used to run back and forth to the water dodging the waves. When the wave would touch your feet, you'd yell "Ahhh it got me, it got me." I don't know who had the most fun, you or me?"

The closer we got to the Pier, the faster we walked. As soon as we hit the old wooden boards, our pace decelerated. We both wanted to savor the time we were going to spend here. We walked arm in arm, watching the kids running around, stopping at the kiosks as we walked by. Then we spotted it at the same time, looked at each other, and chorused, "Funnel Cake." We ran to the line like a couple of kids, back in the day, running to an ice cream truck, after receiving money from their parents.

"Do you still like yours with strawberries just on half?" Mom asked.

My head bobbed up and down. "Yeah. It's perfect like that." We ordered a Funnel Cake to share with strawberries on one half and plenty of powdered sugar all over. We sat at a nearby bench overlooking the beach and watched the children run back and forth dodging the waves. I hadn't realized it until that very moment how much I'd missed

Mom – this mom. We scarfed down the cake and walked the rest of the pier before heading to the Promenade.

Weekends were great at the Promenade. The entertainment was endless. We walked and shopped, mostly window shopping. We heard an old song from Jackie Wilson, "Doggin Me Around." Someone was singing it. Mom stood still trying to locate which way it was coming from. We saw a crowd. She rushed over and fought her way to the front. There were four men and one petite man that tore the song up. Mom yelled, "Oooh, sing the song man." She started moving around swinging her hips from side to side and singing along. She had an angelic voice. The man who'd already gotten most of the women excited was drawn to Mom for some reason. Maybe the way she was gyrating around. I hadn't seen her move like that before. She exuded such self-confidence, like she belonged, knew she was special. While she was dancing around, I took this opportunity to call Matthew to tell him I'd be home late. I didn't want her to hear me change my plans because she'd definitely insist on going back home. I wanted to keep her out as late as I possibly could.

"Hey, baby, what's up?"

"Hi. Since you called me baby, I guess you're not mad at me anymore, huh?

"I'm not mad, but we still need to talk tonight."

"That's why I'm calling. I'm with my mom in Santa Monica so I'm going to be home pretty late."

"Okay. Call me when you're on your way home and I'll meet you there."

"Thanks. Talk to you later." Dang, what made him think I still wanted to talk to him tonight? Oh well, I guess the least I could do was stay up and talk after almost getting the man killed today.

That man singing was getting a little too close to Mom. I'd better get back over there. I couldn't believe she just hugged that strange man. I wiggled my way back through the crowd and grabbed her hand. "Let's go, Mom."

"Mom? I know this fine woman can't be your mother?" The singer was holding her hand, and Mom was standing there smiling like a schoolgirl happy to finally be noticed by the high school quarterback.

I stood in front of him. "She can be and she is. Now move." I moved his hand from hers. "Let's go, Mom." She picked up her bags and waved a flirtatious good-bye.

"Now that man knows he was singing that song. I hadn't heard that song is so long," Mom said jovially.

"You were having a little too much fun over there."

"That's what we're supposed to be doing today, having fun, remember?"

"Are you getting hungry?" It'd been hours since we had eaten half our salads and the funnel cake we shared about an hour ago seemed to only wake up my appetite.

"Yes, I'm starving. I want to sit outside wherever we go."

Not only was she self-confident, she was getting a little pushy. I couldn't remember ever seeing her speak up and say what she wanted. She was always answering how she knew my father wanted her to answer. She could be so happy if she'd just get up enough courage to leave him.

Maybe when all three of us confronted her, we'd be able to convince her to leave him. She still had a lot of life left in her, but if she stayed with Dad, he'd surely suck the rest of it out of her.

When I called Matthew, I noticed I had four missed calls from Dad. I'm sure he'd tried to call Mom, but with all the noise she probably didn't realize he'd been trying to call. Or by the way she was looking at old Cool Daddy singing that song, maybe she just didn't care Richard had been calling.

"Let's go there." Mom spotted a nice little Italian restaurant in the center of the Promenade with tables outside so she wouldn't miss a thing. I wouldn't trade this day for anything in the world. The only thing that could have made this day better was if Jerome and Jaden were here to share it with us.

We were seated immediately at the table closet to the street. We ordered two different pasta dishes so we could sample each other's plate. Then Mom surprised me again by ordering a bottle of wine. *Who is this woman?* We ate, drank, and talked for hours. I think the waiters wanted us to leave. We had been there for close to an hour after we'd paid the bill. We finally tore ourselves from our seats and slowly paced our way through the crowds back to the car. The closer we got to the car, the exuberant personality she'd shown for the past several hours dissipated. The joy I'd witnessed in my mother's eyes slowly began to disappear. It looked like she was walking her last mile; her death sentence had finally come. When we got to the car, all her energy had faded.

Chapter Nineteen

We arrived at Mom's about thirty-five minutes later. We walked in to a dark house. The glow from the television led us to the family room where my father still sat, but now with a half-empty bottle of liquor.

"Richard, we're back."

"So, that's supposed to mean something to me now?"

Mom gestured for me to speak. "Hi, Dad." All I got was a grunt.

"I guess neither one of you know how to answer your phones. I guess that's just if I'm the one calling. I bet you guys answer when other people call." His words were slurred.

"Richard, it was noisy where we were. We just didn't hear our phones." Mom stood at the side of the chair trying to pacify her husband. This was something I'd observed her doing for years. I was very acquainted with the routine that was about to take place.

"You must think I'm stupid. Do you think I'm stupid?" He spun around looking up at Mom like a panther about to leap on his victim. I wanted to take her away, but I knew she'd stand by her man. He'd probably make her feel guilty for enjoying her life for just a little while today.

To my surprise, for the second or third time today, my mother turned away from my father and looked at me. "Princess, I had a wonderful time. We should do it again soon." She took a couple of strides towards me and gave me a big hug.

This took my father's anger to new heights. He tore from his chair and jumped in Mom's face. "You don't leave this house and stay out all day and come in and out of here when you feel like it. You answer to me!" He shook his hand in her face as if he were scolding his misbehaved child.

"Dad, calm down! We just went shopping and out to eat. She left you a note."

"I don't care about no note. She doesn't go running around here like she's some single woman staying gone all day." He growled like a newly-caged animal looking for someone to devour. Mom gazed up at Dad with a possessed evil, sort of like the little girl in that movie *The Exorcist*. She didn't blink. His ranting didn't seem to faze her at all.

Her silence broke when she slowly turned from him and smiled at me. "I'm going to bed, I'll call you in the morning." She walked away.

Dad started after her, but I grabbed his arm. "Why are you so angry with her? Why are you always so angry with her?"

He jerked away from me and went back to his king chair. "She knows we don't do things like that around here. She doesn't just leave without telling me and stay gone all day."

"You mean leave without asking your permission. She's your wife, not your child."

"See, that's what you don't understand. A wife is supposed to check with her husband…"

"I understand checking out of respect for your marriage, but that's not what I see in your relationship with Mom. And if that's the case, why don't you have to check with her when you're going out to hang with your friends, which by the way, are mostly single men?"

"Who do you think you're talking to? I don't have to answer to you."

"That's the problem. You don't have to answer to anyone, but you expect everyone to answer to you. Where's the mutual respect? Can't you see how sad Mom is? Haven't you noticed she never smiles?"

"I hate to burst your bubble, but your mother smiles a lot around here. I'll stop you now before you start in on all that black and white crap. You seem to be stuck on color way more than me. You're always trying to act like I treat your mother a certain way because she's black, but it's not that. As a matter of fact, it's your black men out there that don't respect black women. Why aren't you ever talking about that? Most of them desire every woman, except the black ones, but you're always hammering on me like I'm the bad guy. If you really want to know the truth of the matter, the time when I see your mother sad is when you've been around. While you're so busy trying to make me out to be the bad guy, you need to evaluate yourself, young lady. You think you know everything, but you don't. Maybe that's why you can't keep a man. Maybe you need to tone down that high and mighty attitude and stop being so opinionated."

I decided it was time for me to leave. I couldn't take this anymore. It made no sense trying to argue with a drunken man. "All I know is I watched my mother showing more happiness today than I've seen in at least the past fifteen years. For the record, I have a man. A wonderful man that respects me and my opinions."

He glared at me. "The only reason that black man is so into you is because you're half white. Don't fool yourself."

I couldn't believe him. I stormed out of the house. I sped home so pissed off I forgot to call Matthew. When I made it home, I poured myself a glass of wine to calm myself down. Just as I removed my shoes and slouched down into my chaise in my room, my cell phone began vibrating. I checked Caller ID. It was Matthew. "Hello."

"Hey. You and your mom still out?"

"No. I just got home."

"I thought you were going to call me when you were on your way?"

"I forgot. I…"

"I'm on my way. See you in a few minutes. Bye."

How does he know I still want him to come over here?

Matthew rang the bell in just enough time for him to speed from Los Feliz to Hollywood. He must have been standing at his front door when he called. I jumped up and rushed to the door. "Hi."

"Hey, baby." He stepped in and swept me up in his arms and kissed me as if he hadn't seen me for months. His body, pressed next to mine, felt so good. I didn't realize how much I needed to see Matthew. We went to the bedroom. I undressed and hopped into the shower. Matthew joined me. After playing in the shower, we climbed into bed. We both had to work early the next day. I was happy he hadn't brought up the earlier events because I just wanted to sleep and forget most of the day. As we cuddled up, he said, "You know we still need to talk about today."

I let out a deep sigh. "Can we please talk about this tomorrow? I'm really tired. I know you're still bothered, but I need to go to sleep. I promise I won't put you in that kind of situation ever again."

He turned over and climbed on top of me. "I want you to bother me. I want to be involved. I just don't want you to put yourself in any danger. I'm not worried about me. I'm worried about you." He pressed down and kissed me. "I care about you. I love you."

That came as a shock. *Why was he in love with me? Why so fast?* Before I knew it, I blurted my thoughts out aloud. "Why do you love me? Is it because I'm half white? Is it because of my light eyes and my silky long hair? Why are you in love with me?" I snapped.

"Excuse me? Why in the hell would you say something like that? I thought I loved you because you were a strong, beautiful, smart black woman. I thought I loved you because you had a wonderful personality, because you had a great sense of humor and a caring heart. I thought I loved you because you were driven, confident, and trustworthy. But most of all, I thought I loved you because you knew who you were and you loved yourself. But I can see now I was clearly wrong. You're just another confused woman. I'm outta here." He said all of this while snatching his clothes and shoving his legs in his pants. He snatched his keys off the nightstand and ran out before I could get a word in edgewise.

I ran after him. "Matthew, wait, wait. I didn't mean it like that! Baby, wait, please. I made a mistake!" I grasped his shirt right as he reached the front door.

He turned and stared at me. "No, I'm the one that made the mistake." He snatched the door open and escaped my clutches. I did something I'd never done and never thought I'd do. I ran outside behind him with nothing but a skimpy silk robe on. I wasn't concerned if the neighbors heard me begging. I needed to get my man back.

"Matthew, stop and hear me out, please." I stood outside begging him not to leave. I stood behind his car. "The only way you're leaving is if you run me over." He stepped out of the car. I ran over to the driver's side and pleaded for him to come back into the house.

He grabbed me close to him and yelled, "What the hell is wrong with you? Have you lost your mind? I don't know who you are. I fell in love with a strong black woman regardless of your light skin or your light eyes. Now I see I was wrong. You're just a confused little white girl. Look at you. Out here in the middle of the night half dressed making a scene. This must be the white side of you coming out 'cause classy sistahs don't act like this." He shoved me away from him. "Go in the house, Britt."

Tears flooded my cheeks. I knew I shouldn't have questioned his love the way I did, but that was no excuse for him to be so cruel. After all, I am just as much a white girl as I am black. I just always identified with my black heritage more so than my white. I pulled myself together just long enough to say, "I am who I am. Not just black or just white." I turned and strolled proudly on the cold hard concrete back into the house. I entered the house and wiped the small pieces of gravel off the bottom of my feet. My body felt heavy as if I were carrying another person on my back. I dragged myself to the couch in the darkened family room. I gazed across the room, noticing all the black art covering my walls. Just above my fireplace was a huge African woman statue inside a beautiful bronze frame. Small African figurines lined my mantle and my wall shelves were covered with family photos and more small statues of African heritage I'd collected from the Bahamas, Jamaica, Aruba, and the many festivals I'd attended. Everything in my house announced to all who entered of my pride for my Black heritage. I was always loved by my mother's family so, of course, I adapted to my black side. I pulled the throw cover over my cold numb legs and leaned my head back onto the armrest of the couch. I sat there for at least ten minutes thinking about everything Matthew had said to me, but mainly remembering the image of his face when I questioned why he loved me. I closed my eyes only to be startled by the doorbell. I hopped up and darted to the door. I peeked through the peephole. I snatched the door open. Matthew stood outside the door glaring back at me. We stared at each other for what seemed like an eternity.

"We need to talk." I opened the door wide and watched him stroll by me heading for the family room. I followed behind reminding myself to be cool, not get hysterical, and most of all listen to what he had to say.

Shivers swept my body, but I was determined not to cry anymore tonight, at least not in front of him. I was cruel, but he was malicious and owed me an apology.

"I think we both said some things we didn't mean, so I didn't want to leave tonight without clearing things up." He stared in my eyes.

"Yes, we did, and I'm so sorry. I don't know what came over me. I've been dealing with a lot lately, but that's no excuse."

"I'm sorry, too. Maybe this wasn't the best time to express my feelings for you. If you think I'm with you because you're half white, you don't really know me at all. Maybe we better slow things down and really get to know each other."

"You want to stop seeing each other? I know you're not with me because of that. I don't know why I said that."

"Brittney, it had to be a thought in your mind for the words to come out of your mouth."

"But I ..."

"Brittney, I don't want to get into this right now. I just need to get out of here and step back for a minute." He stood up and then I stood. He leaned in to kiss me. "I love you. That doesn't change just because I didn't get the response I wanted. I'll call you." I didn't say another word. I walked him to the door. He left without looking back.

Chapter Twenty

I needed to pull myself together after last night because I was tripping hard. One would have thought I was on drugs or something the way I acted. I called Burke Williams to see if I could get an appointment for a Parafango Body Treatment for that morning. They were booked at Sunset but had an opening for eleven at the Torrance location. I called the staff to let them know I was only available today for emergencies. I thought about calling Adrienne to tell her about my night but decided not to. I didn't feel like hearing about how stupid I'd been. I was doing a fine job of beating myself up today. I didn't need any help in that department. I hopped in the car, hooked up my IPod, and blasted some Brian McKnight.

I arrived just in enough time to change or rather get naked, throw my clothes in the locker, and run to the restroom before my therapist came to escort me to the therapy room. I felt numb lying there while the woman gently scrubbed my body with the salt scrub. She asked me to turn over so she could continue the scrub on the front of my body. My moves were robotic. I couldn't stop thinking. First, about Matthew, my mother, my twin brothers, and my father. I kept wondering why we were so dysfunctional. Felt like someone was shaking one of those glass balls with the snow flakes, but it was my head being all stirred up. Thoughts were flying around until I felt hot wax being painted on my leg. "Ouch!"

"I'm sorry, is that too hot for you?"

"No, it's all right. I wasn't expecting it so soon."

"I said, 'here comes the heat.' Didn't you hear me?"

"No. I was in deep thought."

"Well, just relax and go back to your thoughts."

She finished brushing the wax over my entire body and then wrapped me in the heated blankets and started on my mini facial. I wanted to lay there for hours, but I knew my time was almost over. After the treatment I sat in the recliner in the Quiet Room for about forty-five minutes . I was awakened by two women talking way too loud for the spa. They ruined my quiet "me" time. It was definitely time to leave.

I drove through a burger spot and off to the beach I went. I watched the waves while stuffing my face with French fries and a double cheeseburger. I decided to call

Jerome. He was three hours ahead of me so hopefully he was home and relaxing by now.

"Hello." Just hearing his voice put me at ease.

"Hi, little brother," I said teasingly.

Jerome laughed. His laugh was sweet and contagious. "Hey, big Sis. What's going on?"

"Too much. I feel like running away."

"Oh no. Come on. Things can't be that bad. I haven't known you for too long, but you seem to be a tough lady. Tell baby brother what's going on."

It was weird. We'd only known each other for such a short time, but we acted as if we'd been brother and sister all our lives. I felt close to him. "It's not really anything. I just may have messed up the best relationship I've ever had, that's all."

"You mean you and Matthew had your first little fight?"

"Not so little. He told me he loved me and I questioned him about why he loved me."

"That doesn't sound too bad. If a man tells you he loves you, he should be able to explain to you why or what he loves about you. So what's the problem? He couldn't tell you why he loves you?"

"Well, I sort of..."

"Oh boy, you sort of what?"

"I kinda accused him of being in love with me because I'm half white." There was dead silence on the phone for at least five seconds.

"Excuse me? Has he given you any reason to think that's the reason he's with you? Because, truth be told, some men do date women or tend to prefer women who are of the lighter persuasion. From what you've told me so far about Matthew, I didn't think he was like that. He seemed to be proud of who he is. If he's one of those self-hatred brothers, it's probably best you found out now."

"No. He's not like that at all. He told me exactly what he loved about me and it had nothing at all to do with my light skin or straight hair. I felt like a fool. I knew he wasn't like that. I just let something Dad said get to me. I ended up making a fool of myself and hurting Matthew in the process."

"If Matthew loves you, he's not going to let you go over that. Give him a couple of days to cool off. Then call him and go over to his place and whip it on him." We both burst out laughing.

"You're not supposed to tell your sister to do that."

"Girl, we're all grown. You know what you need to do to get your man back."

"Hey, are you still coming next week?"

"Yes. Just need to tie some things up." I have a young man I'm trying to keep out of jail. He's a good kid, but was in the wrong place at the right time."

"You love working with young men, don't you?"

"Yep. Just like my big sister. That's amazing you do all you can for troubled pregnant teenagers and I work with the young men. We're definitely blood."

"Yeah. I'll be so happy when you come out here. Oh, I have an address for Jaden. Well, I don't have it in my possession yet, but Mr. Benson does. He wants to find him and talk to him first, but he hasn't seen him yet. We should hear something by the end of this week." We talked for hours trying to still catch up on thirty plus years. I was dying to know everything about my brothers. Jerome and I discussed mainly the present, but he had mentioned that his childhood was not something most people could stomach well. He told me he'd explain later. I wanted to know. I needed to know. So I asked. "Jerome, what happened to you when you were a child? I mean, what kind of childhood did you have? I know you grew up being bounced around from foster home to foster home, but what did you mean when you told me most people couldn't stomach what happened to you?"

Jerome chuckled. "Well, I experienced a lot of verbal, physical, and mental abuse through the years. You sure you want to hear this now?"

"Yes. Unless it's too painful for you to talk about?"

"Naw, Sis. God has carried me through those storms. I discuss my past often in hopes of helping others who feel hopeless."

"Oh, that's right. You're involved with the mentoring program at your church, too, huh?"

"Yeah, so I'll tell you how a routine day may have been in one of the homes. We'd be awakened in the morning by someone yelling, 'Get yo raggedy ass up and come and eat yo food so you can get the hell out of here and take yo dumb butt to school.' Then we would get shoved out the door after a few dips of oatmeal, grits, or cold cereal. That was the good part of the day. When we returned home from school, this is when I was about seven and living with the Wilson family, Ms. Wilson would have chores ready for us as soon as we hit the door. Don't get me wrong. Nothing is wrong with doing chores. All kids should do them, but my chore was to wash her nasty crusty feet. She walked around barefoot all day and when I got home, I had to wash her feet. She'd always have on a dress, too short, and with no panties on. I don't know if she ever bathed because ol' girl was funky. She would purposely have her legs open and insist I rub the lotion up her thighs. I guess my facial expression, no, I know my facial expression showed her she was disgusting so she'd get mad at me for that and try to slap the look off my face. It would happen every single weekday. I rubbed ol' girl's legs, looked at her with pure disgust, and got the crap beat out of me for not liking it."

"Wait a minute. Are you saying she beat you every day for that?"

"Yes, but that would just be the routine beating. I was beat for more things. One day she and Mr. Wilson argued in the morning, I knew I was going to get it when I came home from school. I went through the usual routine with the feet, but this time she slapped me so hard I must have flown at least five feet across the room. While I was still on the floor, she got up and plunged towards me and started stomping me over and over again yelling, 'You don't think I'm good enough for you, either, you little ungrateful bastard. No one wanted you. That's why you're here. You think you're too good for me? Turning your nose up at me. Who in the hell do you think you are?' This is the clean version. The things that came out of her mouth that day are unrepeatable in the presence of a lady. Then she put her big size ten foot on my neck and held me down. It seemed like an eternity. That little outburst of hers actually helped me get out of that home."

"How?"

"Now I had visible bruises. She couldn't hide that one. All of the other times she beat me with the chain, or this piece of wood she liked to use, no one could see the bruises. Those slaps across the face weren't really visible either. When you're a child and that's all you know – abuse – you don't tell because you're not sure if the next place is going to be worse. Trust me, the people are usually brainwashing you to feel that way, too."

"Even if the bruises weren't visible before, it seems like with all that beating, especially with a chain, you would have been sick or too weak to function in school."

Jerome laughed. "Sis, those people are masters at abusing without going overboard. Like I said, they have you too afraid to tell anyone because they convince you no one wants you...in my case it was true."

That was the second or third time he said no one wanted him. I couldn't help but feel guilty and even more anger towards my parents for allowing this to happen. I muttered, "Oh."

"You all right?"

"Yeah. Was that the worst home you lived in?"

"No." He laughed. "As a matter of fact, I left there and went someplace even worse. Just like they said I would."

Jerome was quiet for a few seconds. Maybe this was too much for him.

"The next place I went to – sometimes I didn't eat. Sometimes I was locked in a closet, a food closet like a pantry. I was joined by the roaches. The man, Mr. Landers, was the culprit in this home. He hated his life so he wanted to make sure we hated ours, too. Every night, I mean every single night, I prayed God would let me die. I was so angry at God for letting me wake up another day. I thought it was simple enough of a request. I mean back then, I felt no one would miss me anyway, so why can't he let me die? I was constantly called worthless, a piece of crap, again the clean version, an animal because I never smiled. One day I had gone to the store with his wife, she was not as bad, but she was no angel, either. I heard the pharmacist warn her about some medication she picked up. Whatever he said, it made me think that if she took too many, she could possibly not wake back up. All night I wondered how could I get to those pills. We were never in the house alone and we were never allowed in their room or bathroom unless we were cleaning and then someone was usually close by. The next day, while Kenny, one of the other foster boys, was in the restroom, I begged to use their bathroom. I said, 'I have to go bad. Can I please go to your bathroom? Please? It's going to come out.' Normally he would make me go to the backyard. I knew that. Just as he pointed to the yard, I said, 'I have to boo boo. Please, it's about to come out.' I think only because of my theatrics of dancing around holding myself he said 'Go on, boy, but you better hurry up and don't stink up my bathroom too much. As a matter of fact, you stay in there and clean it up.' That was just what I wanted to hear."

"Oh my God, what happened? Well, I know the outcome because you're here, but go on."

"I waited a few minutes then flushed the toilet and turned the water on, full blast, of course, and looked in the medicine cabinet. There were a lot more pills than I thought there would be, so I looked at the ones that said take only one because I thought those would be the strong ones. I couldn't take too many from one bottle, so I took several from different bottles." Jerome chuckled again. "I was ready. This was it. That night Mr. Landers and his friends were all drinking, getting wasted. Those nights were usually long and hard. But for me, I remember this peace coming over me, because I had a plan. This was going to be the last time I had to bear this deplorable burden. I was going to be free of ridicule, insults, name-calling, neglect, the profanity, the verbal and physical abuse – well, as a child I might not have thought these particular things, but this was the end for me. Kenny ran into the room in a severe panic. He was out of breath. He dove into his bed, hid under the covers, shaking. He usually did this when Mr. Landers was on one of his warpaths and looking to beat the crap out of some-one. Before I could go to his side, Mr. Landers burst in the room and launched to Kenny's bed. He ripped the spread off him and started whaling on him. I didn't know what Kenny had done. He didn't usually get that kind of beating. It was usually saved for me. I think because I was the oldest. Kenny was only seven. I found out later Kenny had rolled his eyes at one of Mr. Landers' friends. Anyway, I wondered about sharing some of my pills with Kenny, but I decided not to because I wanted to make sure I had enough. As a nine-year-old kid, I had had enough and was ready to check out. I don't know how I knew this, but I knew that – or rather at the time I thought if you killed someone you didn't get to go to heaven, you went to hell. So that's why I asked God to take me because I knew if I took my own life, I'd go to hell. Although I was in these abusive homes, some of them had us in church weekly, for appearances' sake. But at that point I felt hell couldn't be any worse than what I was living in. I snuck out, tipped to our bathroom, and put the pills in my mouth one by one. I had about ten to twelve pills. I went back to my bed and laid down to close my eyes for the last time. I didn't know how hell would be, but I was ready to face hell rather than one more day at that looney bin. The next day was Saturday. We could sleep a little longer so no one would realize I was dead until around eight o'clock." Jerome exploded into laughter.

"What?" I was on edge listening to these gory details and he started laughing. "What's so funny?"

"I was so freakin' mad when I woke up at seven thirty the next morning. Sis, I was so hurt. Boy oh boy, I couldn't believe my eyes opened and I was in the same room. For a moment I thought, is this hell? But I knew something had gone wrong. I wasn't supposed to open my eyes and see this same old dreary room. We had two twin beds, two very small four drawer chests and a small chair for each of us, the bare necessities for having a foster child. The house was quiet. Kenny was still asleep. I looked around the room and thought, 'Wow, God doesn't even want to be bothered with me.' I knew the Devil took anybody, but God still made the decisions. He was in control of where everybody went. I laid there in that hot room, feeling as if I were in a sweat box. I pulled the cover over my head and cried, trying my hardest not to wake Kenny and especially not to wake up the Landers. Anyway, Sis, I could have you on this phone until the morning with stories of my childhood so I'll have to give you bits at a time."

"Okay, but weren't you sick the next morning? How did you get out of that house?"

"All I remember is feeling funny and tired. Fortunately for me, that's all I felt. If I would have been sick on a Saturday, it would have messed up their day and really pissed them off."

"That's horrible. So how did you get out of there?"

"Mr. Landers almost killed me. I ended up in the hospital. He ended up in jail. I'll tell you that story next time."

"Jerome, with all that you've gone through, do you think you could ever..."

"Could ever what?"

"Love our mother?" I didn't know if I was being too presumptuous to even ask but I did.

"I've thought about that a lot lately. Because I'm a Christian, I believe in forgiveness. I know I have to truly forgive, but I'm human. I've been praying about this daily. Matthew 6:14 says, 'For if ye forgive men their trepasses, your heavenly Father will also forgive you:' Lord knows I need some forgiveness. God has a plan for all of us. I know I had to go through what I went through to get to where I am now. If I hadn't suffered, I wouldn't be able to go out and mentor the hopeless, the suffering, and the abused. I have certain scriptures in my head that keep me up, if you know what I mean. One is 2 Corinthians, 4:9, it says

'Persecuted, but not forsaken: cast down, but not destroyed:' You see God kept me standing for a reason.

When I thought I was worthless and loved by no one, God showed me He loved me. 1 John, We love him, because he first loved us. Even in spite of ourselves. He placed someone in my path that watched over me. Mr. Williams, my guardian angel. He was a wonderful man that taught me about how powerful God is and how I could do all things through Christ who strengthens me. The book of Philippians has carried me too. Anything is possible with God. I'm not sure how I'll feel about our mother yet. I'm just going to continue to pray about it and let Him guide me as I've done for the past sixteen years or so.

"Wow, you really have a lot of faith. In spite of everything you've gone through."

"Yep, faith in God is what got me through all those ugly storms. Are you a religious or spiritual person?"

"Ummm why don't we leave that for another time."

Jerome chuckled. "Uh-oh, will do. With you, it all came easy. I don't know if it's because I always wanted a sister or brother or what, but I've found it easy to refer to you as my sister; to call you Sis. I feel close to you, which has surprised me. It also may have a lot to do with the fact that you didn't know about me and as soon as you found out I was out there, you took action. That means a lot to me. I already love you for that. I don't know how I'm going to feel when I meet her. You're still sticking to the plan, right? You haven't told her you found me yet, have you?"

"No. I'm a little nervous about this. I know she's carried the guilt for not going after you both for many years."

"Let's talk about this when I get there."

"Okay. Well, I'll talk to you later."

"All right, Sis. Later."

Chapter Twenty-One

After Marilyn's pleasant evening with Brittney, she spent the rest of her Sunday night being yelled at by Richard. She was happy the weekend was over, but Marilyn held on to the cheerful memories she had with Brittney yesterday. With Richard gone, the day was pleasant. That would end soon. Richard would be barging through the door shortly, no doubt in his usual barbaric, primitive, malign manner. The doorbell rang.

Marilyn peeked through the peephole. Her hands trembled as she cupped them over her mouth in terror. Her breathing grew deeper and deeper. She feared to open the door, but the impetus to open it was stronger. She flung the door open before she could analyze what would be the best thing to do.

An angry gentleman stood at the door staring straight into her eyes, surprised to see her.

He frowned. "Hi, ummm, I'm looking for the other lady that lives here. I don't know her name, but she's really light and has kind of long brown hair."

Marilyn was so shocked she could barely speak. "My daughter. It sounds like you're looking for my daughter, Brittney. She isn't here."

"Well, ma'am, I don't mean any disrespect to you, but your daughter has been following me around, looking for me, and I don't know why. I followed her here the other night, but I didn't know anyone in this area so I decided to come here today to confront her to see if I could find out what's going on and put a stop to this."

"Please come in. I think I can explain why she was looking for you." The gentlemen walked in and almost immediately tears began to fill Marilyn's eyes.

The gentleman noticed. "Whoa. I don't know what's going on here, but I think I'd better leave. I feel like I'm being set up for something."

"Wait. Please stop." He turned to leave. Marilyn grabbed his arm. "Please, don't go. I'm your mother." As those words came out of her mouth, the emotions poured out behind them. "You're Jaden." She cried.

He backed up. "What the hell are you talking about?"

"You're all grown up, but you still have that same face. A face a mother would never forget regardless of the amount of years that have gone by."

"My mother's dead. She died when I was born." It was as if he was rehearsing a script for a school play.

"I know that's what you were told, but I'm not dead. My husband, your father, forced me to give you and your brother up when you were born."

"My brother?" His eyes arched. "Lady, what are you talking about? I don't have a brother."

"Yes you do. You have a twin brother. Brittney is your older sister."

Jaden shook his head back and forth while waving his hands in front of him. "No, lady, you're old and very confused. Just tell that other lady to stop bothering me. I've been in trouble most of my life and now I'm trying to do the right thing and stay out of trouble. So tell her to leave me out of this mess."

"Wait!" Marilyn yelled. "Please, let me show you. Come with me. I can prove it to you." Marilyn watched him as she guided him to the guest room where she had the pictures of him and Jerome. They stepped into the room. She frantically hurried to the closet searching anxiously for the pictures.

"Lady, you know you shouldn't just invite strange men into your bedroom. You don't know me. I could be a rapist or a killer. You shouldn't be here alone. You're not well."

She came up from the closet with the storage box of photos. "you're no rapist or killer. You're my son. Now sit down. Thank God I didn't let your sister take all of the pictures I had."

At this point, Jaden seemed to decide to patronize the woman and sat on the bed. Marilyn sat beside him with the box in her lap and pulled out a picture from the top of

Jaden when he was born. Jaden didn't react to the picture. "Okay, and?" Then she pulled out a picture of him when he was two years old. He leaned down, studying the picture. He reached for it, taking a curious look.

"I've seen this picture before. I was in nursery school or a day care or something like that. How'd you get this picture of me?"

"A woman that knew the truth helped me keep tabs on my boys. She got pictures for me from time to time." Marilyn revealed pictures of him when he was five, another when he was seven, at age eight, and the last one when he was ten years old.

"Ma'am, this just proves you've stalked me since I was a kid, but for what reason? This doesn't prove to me you're my mother."

"Jaden, you were snatched from me at birth. I'm so sorry I never came looking for you later. I swore I would when I got stronger or when things were better, but things didn't get better and I never got stronger. Please forgive me, Son." She cried hysterically.

Jaden stood up. "I need to get out of here. I'm sorry, lady."

"Please don't go!" Marilyn stood up and wrapped her arms around Jaden, "I'm so sorry. I love you." Jaden seemed to feel pity for the woman and held her to comfort her. As the mother and son embraced, they were startled by a loud noise.

They looked up and Richard stood at the door waving a gun uncontrollably ranting, "You sorry no-good woman. How dare you have some man in my home."

"Wait, Richard, you don't understand. It's not what you think." She knew her husband's bark was worse than his bite, but Jaden also seemed to recognize this look. He saw Richard's badge and knew from the look in his eyes he would shoot first and ask questions later.

Richard took two steps toward them, and Jaden dove for the gun. As they struggled with the gun, Jaden yelled, "This is a mistake. We weren't doing anything."

Marilyn wrestled in the mix of the two big men. "Richard, stop this is our…" There was an ear-piercing explosion. Marilyn clutched her mouth as she watched Richard fall to the floor. His eyes were shocked open. Jaden and Marilyn examined each other, waiting for each other to speak. They knew he was dead.

Jaden's eyes widened with terror while his mouth hung open. "No one will ever believe me. I'm going back to jail. Oh My God, I can't believe this shit!" He clenched his balled fists to his head, slumping over as if he himself had been shot. "Oh My God. He's a cop!" He whimpered and cried, "We have to call someone. We have to call someone now." He straightened himself back to his full upright position.

"No, you were never here. He's already dead," Marilyn said in a trancelike manner. The tempo in her voice changed. "Go. Hurry. I'll take care of this. I let you down once. I promise you, I won't let any harm come to you over this man again. Go!" Marilyn bent down and checked for a pulse, already aware of the obvious. Jaden watched, astonished by her coolness. "You must go, now. Go through the washroom in the back." He was skeptical, but this woman believed he was her son. So he quickly left, following her instructions. He exited through the back door then out of the backyard praying no one would notice him.

Marilyn watched her husband's blood pouring out of his lifeless body. She towered over him before straddling across his sprawled out body to get out of the room. Still in her spell, she glided to the kitchen, picked up the phone and dialed nine-one-one.

"Nine-one-one operator, state your emergency."

"My husband has been shot. I'm at twenty-one fifty Lemolia street in Sherman Oaks."

"Ma'am what's your…"

Marilyn hung up the phone, strolled to the sofa in the living room, and waited.

In about seven to ten minutes, she heard a knock at the door.

"Police department. Open the door."

Marilyn opened the door wide and walked slowly back to the sofa. Neighbors and other police swarmed the front of the house like bees hovering over their honey. The officer studied her as she walked back to the sofa. By this time, detectives had already arrived at the scene. "Ma'am, are you all right? Is anyone else in the house?"

The first Detective, Eddie Henson, had drawn his gun and began inspecting each room starting with the kitchen, followed by the step-down family room, then down the long dimly lit hallway leading to the bedrooms.

The second Detective, Henry Gutierrez, continued studying Marilyn for signs of any physical damage. "Ma'am, are you hurt?" She didn't answer.

"Gutierrez," Detective Henson yelled. "In here."

"Stay here," Detective Gutierrez told Marilyn. "I'll be right back." He ran down the hallway. "Where are you?"

"In here."

He followed the voice. "Oh boy." Gutierrez spotted the body spread out on the floor.

"Call it in. Is the lady still out there?"

"Yeah and Detectives Robinson and Doherty are in the front questioning the neighbor. I think she's in shock." Detective Gutierrez said.

"Yeah, but in shock for what?"

Henson went to check the rest of the house. He reported back there were no signs of forced entry.

Detective Gutierrez proceeded to finish questioning Marilyn while Detective Henson went out to tell the other detectives what was going on. "We have a possible one eighty-seven. Canvas the neighbors to see if they saw or heard anything unusual."

"The husband or the wife?" Detective Robinson asked.

"The husband. Why?"

"Then your victim is probably Lieutenant Richard Adams of the L.A. Sheriff's Department, Compton Station."

"Damn. Everybody better be on their toes with this one. Remember to dot your I's and cross your T's on all reports. I want to turn this over as quickly as possible."

"Yeah, this could get ugly real quick. Please tell me that's the wife in the house and not some other woman."

"She's not talking, but I think she's the wife. Let's get the tape around here so we don't miss or screw up any evidence we may have."

"What's your take on this so far?" Robinson asked.

"Look like she's the perp, but there's definitely a story behind this. He was killed with his own gun at close range. Something's not right. She's tall but too frail to have taken his gun from him and shot him at close range like this. Like I said, something's not right. Let me get back in there and see if Guitierrez has gotten anything out of her."

"Oh, by the way, the neighbor said she's a very quiet woman, keeps to herself, but was really sweet. She thinks she's scared of her husband," Robinson said.

Henson walked back in the house shaking his head. "I have a bad feeling about this one."

"Ma'am, you need to talk to me because this doesn't look good for you. You need to start talking now." Gutierrez was getting a tad annoyed with the silent treatment Marilyn was giving him.

"Hey. Go outside and get some air." Gutierrez gladly got up from the sofa and left the house. The crime scene investigators had arrived and were in the room collecting evidence.

"Marilyn, we spoke with your neighbors. I know you're a nice lady. I also know that's probably Lieutenant Adams lying in the next room. If anything happened and you needed to defend yourself, you need to tell me. Or at least give me a name of someone I can call." She didn't answer. Her tear-filled eyes remained focused on the wall in front of her. "Can you at least tell me for sure that the man in that room is your husband, Lieutenant Richard Adams?"

Chapter Twenty-Two

It was getting late and I hadn't heard from Mom all day, so I decided to go by the house before going home. It was a nice evening. I opened my moonroof and allowed the music to drown out my thoughts. It had been a beautiful relaxing day so the dreadful 405 freeway didn't bother me at all tonight. I exited at Ventura only to find more creeping on the surface streets. Finally, I drove to Lemolia Street. As I continued driving, I noticed bright amber lights flashing from police cars coming from further up the street. As I got closer, I realized the commotion was coming from my parent's house. I felt like all my nerve endings were poking through my skin. Heat rushed my face. The double cheese-burger I had digested a few hours earlier was trying to make its way back up. Could he have killed her? Was my mother dead?

Yellow tape surrounded the house. I drove as close as I could to the house and parked, jumped out of my car, and ran towards the door. I passed two policemen. I think they yelled for me to stop, but I ignored them, yelling for Mom in a panic. A big burly detective standing about six feet tall standing at the door stopped me. I knew most of the detectives, at least in my father's station, but I'd never seen him before. Then I remembered we never lived in his jurisdiction. "Ma'am, this is a crime scene. You can't…"

"This is my parents' house. What happened to my mother?" The detective immediately escorted me into the living room where I saw Mom sitting on the couch. She looked as if she were in shock. Her eyes were empty and lethargic. I rushed to her side, kneeling down beside her. "Mom?" For a second, she looked as if she didn't recognize me. "Mom, are you okay?"

She nodded but still did not speak. I became infuriated. I examined her for scars or bruises. There weren't any. I knew my father was responsible for whatever my mother was going through. "Where the hell is he?" I screamed at the detective, figuring they probably had my father hidden somewhere to protect him. "Where is he?" I turned back towards Mom. "What did he do?"

The detective said, "Ma'am, calm down. I need to speak to you alone." He gestured for me to step away from my mother. "I'm detective Henson, I'm sorry, but I need you to come into the bedroom and identify the body. We believe it's Lieutenant Richard Adams."

Chills swept my body. I grabbed my chest, staring at the detective. I had secretly wished this day would come, but now that it was here, I was daunted by what was possibly waiting for me in the other room. I took a deep swallow as tears began to fill my eyes. Was the man that I both loved and hated really gone? If so, who was responsible? As I walked into the guest room, I quickly noticed a body covered with a large blood-stained canvas. Another detective was stooping over the body while others were scoping the room like the agents from the *CSI* and *Law and Order SVU* shows I'd become accustomed to watching on Sunday nights. They stopped and watched as I walked over to the body. The big burly detective said, "This is the daughter, Brittney Adams."

"Ms. Adams, I'm so sorry we have to do this, but I need you to tell me if this is your father?" The detective held back the bloody canvas revealing only his face.

I felt numb, like someone had ripped my insides out, then relieved that Mom wasn't the one lying beneath the blanket. "Yes. It's him." I finally managed to force the words out.

Detective Henson escorted me out of the room but stopped in the middle of the hallway. "I need to get some information from you. The neighbor called the police after hearing a gunshot. We also got a nine-one-one call from this house, presumably from your mother, saying her husband was shot. When I knocked on the door to question your mother, she let me in, sat on the sofa, and has been there since but hasn't spoken to anyone." The overstuffed detective paused as he waited for me to fill in the missing pieces I obviously didn't have. "I hope you understand the seriousness of this."

I nodded yes, but his tone totally confused me. I provided him with the information he requested: my phone number and address. "Can I take my mother home with me now?"

"Sorry, we need to take your mother to the police station. While there's no evidence of a burglary or forced entry, we believe your mother knows what happened. It appears a domestic situation occurred and your mother may have shot your father."

My legs turned into spaghetti noodles. Could my mother have done such a thing? Why was she so quiet? My thoughts were to protect her at all costs. Deep in my heart, I knew she couldn't and wouldn't kill anyone, especially my father. For some reason, she loved him unconditionally. If she was guilty of this, it was an accident. I didn't want to hear the gory details that night; I just wanted to get my mother out of that house, something I'd wanted to do for years.

"Look, as you already know my father is...was the lieutenant at the Compton Sheriff's Station. If you talk to them, you'll know my mother couldn't have done this. They all know us. They've known us for over thirty years."

"Ma'am, I'm sorry, but I cannot let your mother go until we've finished our investigation."

Detective Henson was a tall, rotund middle-aged man, fitting the stereotype of the typical donut-eating policeman. I knew if I were in trouble, I wouldn't want him to be on duty. "Detective, if my mother can tell you what happened, can she come home with me? I know my mother didn't kill my father. She isn't capable of such a violent act. Besides, she loved him. She is definitely in shock. As a matter of fact, she should be taken to the hospital to be checked out." Detective Henson scratched his thinning, receding hairline. Then he flipped open a clean sheet in his notepad.

"It depends on her statement. We need to know what happened." He appeared already convinced she'd committed this heinous crime.

I walked back into the living room, joining my mother on the flower-printed hunter green sofa to question her; Henson followed closely, seemingly hoping to be a witness to a confession. She was only fifty-seven years old, but she looked to be every bit of seventy tonight. She'd lost a lot of weight in the past several months, more than likely from the stress I'd caused her. Just as I was about to ask my mother the question, chills swept through my body, heat rushed to my face, the hairs stood up on the back of my neck. I knew with all of my being she was hiding something. Her eyes were filled with fear, but not regret. I decided at that moment not to question her in front of the detective.

"Mom, you have to go down to the police station. They need to question you about what happened. I'm going to call a lawyer so I want you to wait and talk to him first. Okay? Do you understand?" She nodded yes and stood up and held her hands towards detective Henson as a sign to be handcuffed. Tears stained her sunken cheeks. I had just recently glimpsed a ray of hope and happiness in my mother the day before. I began to cry as I wrapped my arms around her.

"Did you kill your husband, Mrs. Adams?" My mom continued to cry and never answered. Henson turned to me. "If you know anything about this, you need to tell us. If your mom has nothing to hide, she can just come down to the station for questioning. If she doesn't deny killing your father, I have to assume she did." The detective read my mother her Miranda Rights, handcuffed her, and escorted her to a police car. I followed them out to the car, sobbing while watching them place my mother in the back of a police car like a common criminal. *Mom must have snapped from all of the stress and years of abuse.*

I followed the police car and immediately called Jerome.

"Hey, two calls in one night."

"Jerome" was all I could push out. My voice trembled, my head was spinning, and my stomach was turning flips.

"Brittney? What's wrong? What happened?"

"They're taking Mom to jail." I started crying. I had to be strong in front of Mom, but my fear poured out with Jerome.

"Jail? For what?"

"Dad was shot. He's dead." I began sobbing uncontrollably.

"Brittney. Brittney." He repeated.

"Huh?"

"Where are you?"

"Following the police car. I have to be there with her. She's so scared."

"Brittney, I need you to pull yourself together and tell me what happened. Did she say she shot him? What did she tell the police?"

"That's the problem. She's not saying anything. She won't say a word. That's why they're taking her to jail because no one else was in the house."

"Brittney, if you can get to her, tell her not to say anything until I get there or until I get a lawyer I know to get over there to talk to her."

"No, Jerome. I want you to take care of this. Please come."

"I'm coming on the first flight available. I'll be there, but I don't know how long it's going to take. I don't want her to not be represented. I'm going to make a few calls to see if I can get someone there tonight. Don't worry."

"Okay." I felt better but still felt like throwing up. I couldn't get the image of my mother being handcuffed out of my mind.

"Britt, I have to ask. Do you think she could have done this?"

I didn't know how to answer that. Could she have snapped? Was she capable of killing my father in cold blood? She didn't have any scratches on her as if she'd been struggling.

"That's all right, you don't need to answer that."

"No. I don't think she could do anything like this. I just can't explain it. Please, hurry, Jerome."

"I will. I'll be in touch throughout the night."

I'm met Jerome at nine at LAX. I was so happy when he phoned to tell me he would be there first thing that morning. He couldn't get anyone to bail mom out, so she spent the night in jail. I rolled up to United Airlines right outside of the baggage claim area. I noticed Jerome coming out of the glass double doors dressed to kill or better yet get someone off for murder. I quickly blew the horn and waved my hand out the window. I swerved, almost ramming my front end into someone's rear. I hit the button to open the trunk. He tossed his luggage in the back and hopped in the car.

"Hey, Sis. You okay?" He reached over and hugged me.

"Yes, but I'm worried about Mom. She's never been in jail. I don't know what kind of people are around her. She probably couldn't use the restroom if she had to go in front of everybody. Is it really like that in jail? Is there only one toilet in a room with a lot of people?"

"Whoa. Slow down. I've already made some calls. We'll post bail and get her out of there. A buddy of mine is going to meet us there. It'll make things go more smoothly with a known local attorney handling her case versus an outsider like me."

"You are going to be here the whole step of the way, right? I don't understand this stuff. I need you here."

"Brittney, I'm not going anywhere until this is over. I told David to meet us at the station at ten o'clock. Will we be there by then?"

"Yeah. We should be there in about thirty minutes. Can I go in with you to talk to Mom?"

"No. I'll probably have David go in by himself. You'll see her in the courtroom during arraignment proceedings."

"Where will you be during these proceedings?"

"Waiting outside. I don't want her to see me in the jail or inside the courtroom. We don't need her having any emotional outbursts in front of detectives, the D.A's office, or the judge. We'll have our little reunion outside of that arena."

"I can't believe this is happening. I still have to notify the family of Dad's death."

"Have you had any sleep?"

"I got a couple of hours this morning. I need to get into the house to get insurance information and Mom will need to get her clothes. They said it's a crime scene and I can't go in yet. Can you help me with that? I've never had to deal with anything like this. Planning a funeral and dealing with the court system all at the same time."

"Hey, that's why I'm here. David and I will do everything we can for your mom."

I glared at Jerome. "She's your mom, too." He ignored that comment.

"I'm going to call David to let him know we're on our way. About twenty more minutes, right?"

"Yeah." I was a little perturbed about that comment but was in no position to give him a hard time. Besides, I understood. I knew when he met Mom he'd fall in love with her. She had a loveable personality; everyone loved her.

We arrived at the Century Regional Detention Facility just shy of thirty minutes from the time we left LAX. I turned to Jerome. "This place can't be too bad. This is where they kept Paris Hilton and Lindsey Lohan." Jerome looked at me and shook his head. I wasn't sure why.

I jumped out of the car and began racing towards the door.

"Britt, I told David to meet us in the front of the building."

"I was going to see if someone would go and check on Mom to see if she's all right."

"Sweetie, no one in there is going to do that for you. Come here." He pulled me close to him and held me. "You've been through a lot in one night. You lost a parent and have the other parent in jail. I know you're anxious, but I need you to follow my lead on this, all right?" He slightly pushed me back to study my face. "Got that?"

After staring in a trancelike manner, I finally answered, "Yes."

"Hey, Jerome." An older white gentleman with a dark Hugo Boss looking suit walked up to us.

"David, hey man, thanks for coming on such short notice. This is my sister, Brittney. Britt, David Cohen." I shook his hand but didn't really have time for formalities. I wanted to run inside and get my mother out of jail.

"Hello, thanks for coming," I mumbled.

"Don't look so gloomy." David smiled.

My eyebrows immediately shifted up. Jerome wrapped his arms around me. "My sister's very worried. She has never dealt with anything like this before."

"I totally understand. Let's go get her out of here first, then see what, if anything, the D.A.'s office has on her. Marilyn Adams, right?"

"Right," Jerome answered.

We all walked in, but Jerome and I stayed in another part of the building while David checked in to see Mom.

Michele L. Waters

I felt like my legs were going to collapse out from under me. I was getting light-headed. Jerome tried to comfort me by explaining what to expect. It was like I was hearing the teacher on those Charlie Brown cartoons. "Wonk...Wonk...Wonk...Wonk..." Then I heard a familiar voice.

"Britt." I turned around and saw Matthew rushing towards me. I think he reached me just in time. I felt as if I were going to drop. He provided me the strength I needed to withstand. He held me tight. I held him even tighter.

"How did you know I was..."

"Adrienne called me this morning. Why didn't you call me last night?"

"Everything happened so fast. I didn't know if you wanted to hear from me."

He held my face close to his and kissed me gently on my lips and gazed at me. "Listen to me. I love you. I'm going to be right here for you." I cried. He wiped my tears and wrapped his arms around me.

"Oh, I'm sorry." I pulled back from Matthew. "This is my brother, Jerome." I wiped my face and pointed to Matthew. "This is Matthew."

They shook hands and said simultaneously, "I've heard a lot about you." They both chuckled.

About forty-five minutes later, Matthew and I were in the courtroom waiting to see Mom. She walked in without handcuffs and stood next to David. Everything went so fast. It was like a blur. There were a few what say yous, and then bail was set for two hundred and fifty thousand dollars. I knew I had to come up with ten percent of the set bail;

224

that's about all I knew. One thing my father made sure of was we had a family emergency fund we all had access to. I guess he wasn't so bad after all. I was rushed through paperwork and processing. Everything appeared Greek to me. I felt like I was in a foreign country.

Finally, Mom walked out of a door. We embraced each other for a long time, weeping. I pushed her back and stared at her for a few minutes; I guess to make sure she hadn't been brutalized in any way. We turned around and walked out. Before we got to where Jerome was standing, I looked at her. "Mom, I need you to meet someone else, another lawyer who'll be assisting David in defending you." I held her hand and walked straight to Jerome. She was looking at me so she didn't see him until she was right in front of him.

She looked up and grabbed her chest with one hand and reached to touch him with the other. "Oh, my son." She cried. Jerome held his hands towards her, and she melted into his arms, crying uncontrollably. Jerome tried to fight back the tears, but he couldn't hold back the emotional reunion. Mom looked back up at him. "I'm so sorry. I'm so sorry. Please forgive me." Then she buried her head in his chest, crying uncontrollably.

He rubbed her back. "It's all right."

David broke up the reunion by suggesting we go somewhere more private.

Jerome decided to ride with David so they could talk shop talk before they stopped at my house. They followed me home so I could also have some alone time with Mom.

As we rode, I questioned Mom about what happened. She ignored me by asking her own questions.

"I didn't know you'd found Jerome. Why didn't you tell me?"

"It was going to be a surprise. I wanted to wait until I found Jaden, too. So I could reunite you with both of them together."

"So you haven't found Jaden?"

"No, but he's very close. Right now, I need to redirect my focus to you. Mom, this is very serious. You could end up spending a lot of time in prison, not this little holding cell you were in last night. You could do hard time. When we get to the house, you have to tell Jerome and David every single detail." I looked across at her. "No matter what happened. Tell them the truth."

"We struggled with the gun and I shot him. That's all that happened."

I let out a long hard sigh. "No, that's not all that happened, because it doesn't make sense. Dad didn't just come home and have his gun out for no apparent reason."

"Yes, he did. Were you there?" She gave me a cold piercing stare as a warning not to ask her again.

We arrived at my house around one thirty. Everyone was starving. We had a lot to do, but we were all anxious to get the truth out of Mom so we'd know what we were working with. I threw some burgers on my George Foreman grill and placed condiments, cheese, lettuce, onions, and tomatoes on the kitchen island for buffet style eating. I already had a large pitcher of sweet tea so I placed that on the counter as well.

"Marilyn, I'm going to have to leave pretty soon, so I need to go over your story again. I think you need to understand that as your attorney, there's a thing called attorney-client privilege which means…"

"I'm not stupid, sweetie. I know exactly what it means. We struggled with the gun and I shot him."

David rubbed his chin and gazed over at Jerome. He got off the barstool. "Jerome, can I talk to you for a second?"

The two men walked out to the patio and closed the glass door behind them. I watched them having this conversation that could possibly determine the plan to defend my mother of murder while she sat at the table acting as if she didn't have a care in the world. I felt hopeless. What was she hiding and why hide it from me? Her own daughter. Shortly they walked back in.

"Mrs. Adams, I'll be in touch with Jerome and with you a little later, but I need to warn you. If you don't tell me the whole truth, that will make my job much harder in defending you. The D.A.'s office is taking it easy on you because you called nine-one-one, you didn't flee, and you appeared to be in shock. They are charging you with second degree murder only. This still has a punishment of up to twenty-five years in prison. Please think about that. We need your help to defend you." Mom glared at him motionless and still seeming unconcerned. He let out a long aggravated breath. "Ok, I'm out of here. Mrs. Adams, I'll be in touch."

"Wait," Mom yelled. We all had a gleam in our eyes in hopes she was ready and willing to tell us what happened. "You said we have an attorney-client privilege which I fully understand, but if Britt and Jerome are called to testify, they're sworn to tell everything they know, right?"

I immediately jumped my non-law educated self into the mix. "I would never say anything that would convict you of murder."

"Your mother's correct. You may not have a choice if the prosecuting attorney has knowledge of something and asks the right question and you answer falsely, you would be committing perjury. Jerome, on the other hand, is the second seat, so he has the same attorney-client privilege as we have. Is there something else you'd like to disclose to me in private?"

"No. I was just wondering."

Our hope was puffed up then immediately deflated by her actions.

Chapter Twenty-Three

A few hours later we met a detective at the house to escort us in to get the insurance policies, address books, and clothes for Mom. We had been so busy trying to defend Mom we hadn't had time to mourn our loss. Or maybe Mom had cried last night in jail. When we walked in, I noticed an unpleasant smell that filled the entire house. The smell of death.

"I need to get something out of the dryer." Mom told the detective. "It's by the back door. Is it okay to go there?"

"Yes."

I heard her but wasn't paying much attention. I retrieved the box in their bedroom closet and took out what I thought to be the current journal of insurance policies, credit card numbers, and pertinent emergency information. This was the emergency journal, but I wasn't sure if it was the most current one. I knew it was usually updated either annually or semi-annually, whatever was appropriate. I walked into the utility room where I saw Mom standing studying the black dust on the knob of the back door. "Mom?" She jumped.

"Yes, Britt."

"Why were you staring at that door like that? Are you all right?"

She clutched her chest. "Yes. I'm just feeling a little overwhelmed right now. Did you get the emergency journal?"

"I think so. Is this the most current one?"

She checked the inside of the front cover at the date . "This is it. I'll get a few clothes and then be ready to leave."

Jerome had already left the house and waited for us outside. When we came out, Jerome sat Mom in the front seat and made sure she was strapped in. Before I could get to the driver's seat, he called me over to the back of the car. "That lady over there keeps staring at me." He looked over to the left towards Ms. McFee's house. "Maybe she remembers something that she hadn't told the police."

"Let's go talk to her." I reached in and placed the keys in the ignition to turn the AC on. "Mom, we'll be right back. Are you all right in there?"

"Yes, but where are you going?"

"Just over to Ms. McFee's to tell her to watch out for the house because no one will be here for a while."

"Oh, okay."

We began walking towards Ms. McFee's house. She turned to her plants, pretending not to see us coming her way. "Hello, Ms. McFee."

"Oh, hello, Brittney. I'm so sorry to hear about your father. How's Marilyn holding up?" Although she was talking to me, she suspiciously watched Jerome.

"She's doing well under the circumstances, I guess. But...Ms. McFee?" I had to call her name again to get her attention off Jerome. "This is Jerome." I decided I'd better keep his identity hidden until I got some information.

Jerome extended his hand, "How are you, ma'am?"

"I'm good. Thanks." She frowned, forcing a fake weak smile, still studying his face.

"Ms. McFee." She finally looked at me. "Did you happen to see anyone over here yesterday? Someone around my parents' house you hadn't seen before?" She was the nosiest neighbor on the street. There was always that neighbor that knew everyone's business and ran their mouth entirely too much but we needed that person and I was looking right at her.

"As a matter of fact, I did."

"Really? Can you give us a description of him?" Jerome asked.

She leaned back, folded her arms, staring at Jerome then back at me. "I think I need to talk to you in private, Brittney."

"Ms. McFee, he's a long-time friend of the family and a lawyer. It's fine to talk in front of him."

Ms. McFee turned her back to us. "I'll talk to you at another time then."

"Wait." I turned to Jerome. "Why don't you go and check on Mom."

"No problem. It was nice meeting you, Ms. McFee."

"Yeah, right," she mumbled.

"All right, who did you see?"

"The man that just walked away was the man I saw yesterday. He looked a little different; a tad darker, with a scraggly-bearded face. He's just clean today." Ms. McFee crinkled up her mouth.

"He just got off of a plane from Maryland this morning, so it couldn't have been him. So, the man looked like him."

"Well you know what they say, we all have a twin somewhere. His was here yesterday a little before I heard that gunshot. The shot that killed your father."

"Thank you, Ms. McFee. Please watch the house for us. Thanks." I couldn't get to the car fast enough. Jerome was bent down by the passenger's seat talking to Mom. When he noticed me coming, he stepped around to the back of the car. I didn't want Mom to get suspicious, so I quickly whispered, "Jaden was here."

We got into the car and headed back to my house to start making funeral arrangements. I wanted to get Mom busy so I could talk to Jerome privately.

"Mom, you need to call Aunt Libby right away. I should have called her this morning but things were way too crazy."

"Princess, can't you call her? I don't want to talk right now. I didn't sleep at all last night. I really need to lie down."

Even better. "I'm sorry. I wasn't thinking. Why don't you go into your room take a hot bath and try to get some sleep. I'll take care of this." One of my guest bedrooms was a miniature master suite with its own full bathroom, small sitting area, and huge walk-in closets. Mom claimed it as her room whenever Dad allowed her to hang out with me over night. I shut the door behind her and called Aunt Libby before joining Jerome in the family room to begin putting the pieces to this puzzle together. Aunt Libby had a zillion questions, but I told her I needed to fill her in later. I needed her to call her family because I wasn't going to call them.

I peeked in on Mom. She was relaxing in the bathtub. I rushed back to the family room and gestured for Jerome to follow me to my room which was located on the other side of the house. I closed the door, turned the television on, and retreated to the chaise in the sitting area.

"So that's why Ms. McFee was staring at me so crazy. She thought I was there yesterday?"

"Yes. So now we know why Mom isn't talking, but I don't understand how Jaden knew where she was unless he was looking for his birth parents. Why would he kill Dad? Unless Mom told him he forced her to give you guys up and he was angry? This doesn't make any sense. Should we tell her we know he was there? At this point, all we're doing is guessing." Then we heard the newscaster on the television say:

"Breaking News Just In on the homicide case of a Sheriff's Lieutenant Richard Adams. His wife, Mari-

233

lyn Adams, was released this morning on two hundred fifty thousand dollars bail. Her lawyer, David Cohen, said He had no comments at this time. Update on this case at nine o'clock."

We both sat speechless watching the brief news announcement. "Brittney, I know you want to hope or see only the good in Jaden, but we don't know him. As a matter of fact, what little we do know about him is he's been back and forth in jail for petty crimes. What if he's taken his crimes up a notch?"

"What are you implying? This is our brother. Can't we at least give him the benefit of the doubt?"

"We don't know him. Look, I came here to help you keep your mother from going to prison. Now we have to do everything possible to help her or help him. Which will it be?"

"Our Mother. Why can't you get that through your thick skull? She's your mother, too. Stop calling her 'my mother.'" I burst into tears. I was mentally and physically exhausted. Jerome held me.

"I'm sorry, Sis. The last thing we need to do is start snapping at each other. This is hard for me, too. I don't even know what to call her. I've gone thirty-two years of my life not calling anyone Mom. The earliest memories I have of a decent foster parent was with that lady that kept us in church. I called her Nana. I've never had the luxury of calling someone Mom. So bear with me. Give me a little more time. Trust me when I tell you, I'm going to work this case in defending her knowing she is my mom."

I wiped my tears. I knew it was time to get to work. No time for any more emotional outbursts. "I'm going to call Mr. Benson and get that address for Jaden. We have to find him before someone else does."

"I'll call David and fill him in. Maybe he can come pick me up so we can talk to some of the investigating detectives."

I got the address from Mr. Benson and the street sounded familiar, but I didn't know why. Matthew called just as I hung up with Mr. Benson.

"Hey. How are you doing? Has your mom given you any more information on what took place yesterday?" Matthew asked.

"No, but we might have a breakthrough. I just spoke with Mr. Benson and I got the address, so I'm going to go over there and see if I can find Jaden."

"What does Jaden have to do with anything?"

"A neighbor saw him over there yesterday. We think that's why Mom isn't talking. She's hiding something and it has to do with protecting her son."

"Did you ask her about it?"

"No, not yet. Anyway, I have to go. Are you coming over now?"

"No. That's why I was calling, to let you know it'll be late when I get there."

"Ok. Jerome might meet up with David to discuss the case this evening and I'll go look for Jaden."

"Let me speak to Jerome."

"Why?" I snapped.

"I just want to speak with him for a minute."

I handed the phone to Jerome. "It's Matthew."

"Hey, Matthew, what's up?"

"I got it. Not a problem. It was good talking to you. I'll see you later."

Jerome handed the phone back to me. I guess they had to do some male bonding or something. "Hey. What was that about?"

"Nothing just male bonding. I gotta go. I'll see you later," Matthew said. I didn't have time to try to figure out what he was being secretive about. Anyway, I figured Jerome would tell me.

I watched Jerome's face. "What did Matthew want with you?"

"Just checking in to see what's going on and how you're holding up. He seems like a real nice guy." I knew there was more to the story, but I didn't have time to think about it.

"Did you get in touch with David?"

"I left him a voice mail. I remembered he told me earlier he had some event he was going to tonight and wouldn't be available until tomorrow, so I guess I'll be riding with you to find our brother tonight."

Although Mom was probably out for the night, I didn't want her to be alone while Jerome and I were out fishing for our brother. I called Adrienne to come stay at the house while we were out.

"No wonder this address seemed familiar to me. This is the same area we followed the mystery man to," I told Jerome. "You know, the one I told you about that kept coming around talking to one of our residents." I pulled over to an open parking spot across the street from the same building I'd visited just last week. I needed to warn Jerome without freaking him out. "Jerome, I don't want to scare you but…"

"Scare me?" Jerome laughed. "You just make sure you don't go in there and piss anybody off. I'm used to the hood. I grew up in Oakland. The part I grew up in makes your little South Central or Nickerson Gardens look like the suburbs."

"Well, Matthew and I almost got ourselves in a bit of a mess the last time we were here. At least this time we have an address. I just hope we don't run into the guy who told us to never come back."

"Oh, God, let's just get this over with."

For the second time, I walked into this dungeon – looking, drug – infested, thug – filled building. It was worse than I remembered because it was dark. Dimly lit creepy wall sconces barely hung onto the walls. Some were broken with pieces of glass still on the ground beneath the light. We both tiptoed as if we were walking on shells, looking carefully at the faded numbers on the doors. We finally spotted number forty-nine. Both of our eyes widened as we took in a deep breath. We tapped on the door. It wasn't closed all the way, so it opened slightly as we knocked. Again we looked at each other, wondering do we turn around and run or follow through. We chose the latter.

"Hello? I'm looking for Jaden." I leaned into the narrowly cracked open door just enough for anyone in the apartment to hear but low enough not to bring attention from the other residents. No answer.

"Hello?" Jerome called out. "Jaden?" He pushed the door wider and stepped in. It appeared no one was home. All lights were off but the smell of dirty socks, feet, and Fritos all mixed together overwhelmed us. We took another step inside and suddenly Jerome was pushed from the back. A familiar voice said, "Turn around and I'll blow your head off. Put your hands up where I can see them." Jerome and I stood in the dark, smelly apartment with our backs towards some dangerous thug or thugs. We didn't know what to expect next.

"Dude, I don't mean any disrespect. I'm just looking for my brother. His name is Jaden."

"Quit lying. I just saw you guys here last week looking for some made-up character."

"I was not here last week. Let me turn around so you can see my face."

"Maybe she got another Joe to come up in here with her, but I recognize Red here from the back."

"Man, I'm just looking for my brother. Let me turn around."

"I was here last week. I was looking for someone else." My voice trembled.

"Yeah, and I'm boo boo the fool. Turn around, man, slow."

As Jerome begin to turn, I twisted around just enough to see what was going on. After Jerome turned completely around the reflection from the light from the hall right outside the door fell on his face just enough for the man not to deny Jerome's identity. He immediately dropped his hand down to his side. "Damn." Just as he blinked to take a better look, Jaden walked up behind him.

"What's going on, Ant?" He stepped in closer and stood face to face with his brother. "Damn."

"Excuse me?" I still had my hands up with my bottom half still facing in the opposite direction, with the top of my body still twisting to face them. "Can I put my hands down and turn all the way round now, please," I asked sarcastically.

"Yeah, turn around, Red," the young man said. I guess I had a new nickname now.

"Close the door, Ant." Jaden hurried to a light switch on the wall and finally gave us some light. Oh, but how I wish he hadn't. There were clothes and dirty dishes all over the place. A total pigsty. "Sorry for the mess. You know, it's a bachelor's pad." Jaden looked embarrassed.

"No, it's a pig's pen. We can talk about this later," I said.

Jerome laughed and shook his head. "This is your big sister. If you don't have one, this is what you can expect from now on. Like she said, we can talk about that later. Right now we have a lot of more important issues to discuss beginning with what happened yesterday."

"Wait a minute," Ant blurted. "Why didn't you and that other dude just tell me Jaden was your brother when you came last week?"

"I wasn't looking for my brother last week. I was following another guy who just happened to have come into this same building last week."

"No. I saw you following me. That's why I followed you last week to that house. I went to the house yesterday looking for you to see why you were following me."

"Hold on. I was following a man who'd been coming to our home for unwed mothers. This man was talking to my resident Angela." Jaden and Ant both looked at each other deviously. "Oh my God, please don't tell me you're Angela's baby's father. Please don't tell me you raped a sixteen-year-old girl, Jaden."

"Oh hell no!" He raised both hands then dropped his head to the side staring at Ant as if to say "you need to say something."

"I'm her baby's father, but I swear I didn't rape her."

"Well what would you call it when a girl changes her mind and says, 'No.'" I totally forgot this man had pulled a gun on me twice.

"I did not rape her," Ant yelled.

"Is that why you were following me, to get to Ant?"

"Everybody calm down," Jerome commanded. "Let's remember why we're here tonight. Look, that issue is going to have to be placed on the backburner for now. We need to pull a defense together and quick for your mother...our mother."

"You're right," I said. "But I just need to know one thing, Jaden? Why is Angela so upset every time you leave?"

"I guess she gets upset because she doesn't want to talk to Ant. Oh, by the way, this is my cousin Anthony Hughes. I keep telling her they need to talk about this. He thought she wanted him – that they were on the same page, until she didn't want to talk to him anymore afterwards. My cousin is no rapist. You don't know him but I've known him all of his life. He's no rapist."

"Like I said, let's table this conversation for another day. Please," Jerome reminded us again.

I didn't experience that warm gushy feeling with Jaden like I had with Jerome, but he was still my brother. "Okay, Jaden, we need to know what happened yesterday at Mom's. The truth. Every single detail." Jaden once again looked to Ant and then to Jerome, seemingly unsure if he should or could trust us.

"Look, it was an accident and the lady..."

"Your mother," I said.

"Yeah. She told me to leave and she would take care of it. There was nothing I could do because he was already dead. I thought she was a little off, so I didn't think anyone would believe me if I told them she had invited me in. I mean it looked real bad for me, and I already have a record. He was a cop so I just ran. I swear, we both tried to explain to him we weren't doing anything wrong. I think he thought we were messing around."

"Wait a minute. Slow down, man," Jerome said. "We need details from the time you walked up to the door until the time you left. We know her husband..."

"Your father," I interrupted.

Jerome looked at me with contempt. "Don't push it, Brittney. This is the man that forced my mother to give me away at birth because he didn't want any black boys so he's going to be the man, her husband, the jerk, or the asshole, take your pick."

"She didn't tell me that part yesterday. What do you mean because we were black? You mean he was married to a black woman but was a racist son of a..."

"Hold it. This is our sister and we'll respect her. The man was her father, so let's not go there. At least not now. We'll talk later," Jerome told Jaden.

"I'm sorry." Jaden shifted his eyes at me and then quickly back to Jerome. "I'm so confused right now. I got pieces of a story floating around in my head." He looked back at me. "Excuse my manners. Do you want something to drink? Have a seat. Looks like we have a lot of catching up to do."

"No. I'm not thirsty. Thank you." I was thinking if I hadn't had anything to drink in the past week, I still wouldn't drink out of that dump. I guess Jerome noticed my discomfort.

"Are there any lounges around here where we could go? Maybe to get some drinks, relax, and talk?"

"Lounges? The spots I hit up are more like clubs. They're loud. Not a place to talk."

"Oh. I know a place not far from here on Sunset. It's an Indian restaurant but it has a very nice lounge. I don't remember the name of it but I can take us right to it."

"Sounds like a plan. Do you need to change?" Jerome asked Jaden.

"No. I'm good." *No this negro didn't.* Jaden sported dingy jeans, not fashion dingy-looking jeans, but dingy as in have you had these on for the last five days. He topped it off with a wrinkled T-shirt and an oversized worn-out sweatshirt. "Hey, why do you need all of these details from me anyway. You're her daughter. Didn't she tell you what happened?"

"No. Mom hasn't mentioned you. She's trying to protect all of us by keeping your presence a secret. So we need to figure out how to keep her out of jail without implicating you as well. I'm no lawyer, but that's the direction we're heading, right?" I looked to Jerome for approval. "By the way, your twin here is a lawyer. So you're in good hands, but you have to be straight with us."

"Well, this sounds like a bunch of family business, so I'll holla at you later." Ant grabbed Jaden's hand and pulled him towards him and gave him a solid side chest bump. Then he shook Jerome's hand. "Nice to meet you." He stepped towards me. "Nice to meet you, too, Red." Then leaned in. "I didn't rape her. I would never hurt Angie like that. I hope we can talk once you get things straight with your mom."

I held my hand out to shake his. "We'll talk very soon. I'll get your information from Jaden."

I escaped the dungeon once again. We arrived at the Indian restaurant in ten minutes. It's amazing how different one part of the same city can look just minutes apart from one another.

Thank goodness it was a weeknight. We had our choice of seats in the lounge.

"I don't mean to be a jerk about all this, but just because your mom kept a lot of pictures of us as kids and she lost her boys at birth, how do you know for sure we're your brothers? I mean it's kinda obvious we're brothers." He switched his finger back and forth between him and Jerome. "How can you be sure we're your missing brothers?"

Jerome and I cut our eyes at each other and giggled. "We already had a DNA test performed. She's definitely my sister which makes her your sister."

"Wow. Man, this is a lot to take in. In two days I learn my mother and father were both alive. Now I'm responsible for the death of my father." Jaden rubbed his head then covered his face with his hands before they dropped to his lap.

When Jaden put it out there like that, the mood became solemn and dismal. Jaden immediately went into the details of the day before from the time he knocked on the door to the time he ran out the back door. We finally had the whole story. Jerome called David, left him a message giving a quick summary of our new information, and asked if he could meet us first thing in the morning.

"We're going to have to confront…our mother." Jerome had a sudden jolt of my reminders and started laughing. "I'm trying, lady. I'm trying." He was so sweet.

"Why don't you call her Marilyn for now?" I finally conceded to his inability to see her as I'd seen her all my life.

"Thank you, because I wanted to say Mrs. Adams, but I didn't want to see you have a hissy fit."

"I know we're going to have to confront her but not tonight. She needs her rest. "Jaden, are you working? I mean, are you available to come over tomorrow to my house? I think it's time for a complete reunion."

"Yeah, I can come. It's a little hard for me to get full-time work, so I go to Labor Ready everyday to get work. There hasn't been anything for the past two days, so I can take care of this tomorrow. Besides, the dispatcher told me a job might be coming up next week. I'd rather take care of this now."

I had a strong feeling Jerome wanted to speak to Jaden alone, so I excused myself to go to the restroom to give them a moment. I fiddled around in the restroom longer than I needed. On my way back to the couch, it appeared Jerome was in a deep, serious conversation with Jaden. Jaden was leaning in catching every word. Jerome spotted me and stopped the discussion. I pretended I hadn't noticed the sudden change in their manner.

When I sat down, my cell started vibrating. I checked the screen. It was Matthew. Time had slipped by so fast. "Hi."

"Hey. Where are you?"

"We're at that Indian place on Sunset. We have my brother Jaden with us."

"Really? So you finally got both of your brothers. Well, I'll let you catch up tonight and maybe I'll just see you tomorrow."

I wanted to see Matthew tonight, but I didn't want to seem desperate or needy. "We were about to head home in a few minutes."

"I can still come over tonight. I just figured you'd probably want to have this time alone with them. Without the boyfriend hanging around, but hey, if you want me to come, I..."

"I want you to come." I turned slightly and whispered, "I was looking forward to seeing you tonight."

"Say no more. I'll be there. Is your mom there alone?"

"No. Adrienne is there with her until we get back."

"I'll head over there now. I'll see you when you get there."

"All right, Bye." I loved my brothers and was happy to see them, but I needed my man tonight. "We better get out of here. It's getting late, and I don't know what Adrienne's schedule is like tomorrow. I need to get back."

We dropped Jaden back at his apartment building after Jerome and I saved Jaden's information in our cell phones and Jaden did the same with ours. Jaden promised he'd be at my house at ten o'clock in the morning.

On the way home, Jerome was quiet. "Is anything wrong?"

"No. I'm just feeling a little overwhelmed. All these years and I find out I have a great sister and Jaden's a little rough around the edges but he's a good guy. He's really trying to get his life together. He and his father are not close at all, and he thinks his mom feels obligated towards him. It's just amazing."

When I pulled up, I spotted Matthew's car parked across the street. I had been so high strung for the past two days. I wanted to melt in his arms all night. I couldn't get into the house quick enough. I got everyone situated in their rooms. Adrienne decided to sleep over since it was so late. Matthew had to leave early in the morning for a court appearance for one of his parolees. We rushed to my room.

"You know I'm nosy. What were you and Jerome talking about on the phone earlier?

He chuckled. "You are nosy." My crinkled face told him I still wanted to know. "Okay." He pulled me close and wrapped is arms around my waist. "I told him not to let you go find Jaden alone because you were already warned that he was living in a dangerous area but you could be a little hard-headed. That you'd been a little sheltered and didn't know when to be afraid and back off. I just wanted to make sure you were safe."

"Still trying to keep me safe, huh?"

"That's my job." He kissed me passionately. His loving was just what my tense body needed.

Chapter Twenty-Four

Aunt Libby always rented her own car when she came to visit. I was glad this time was no different because I didn't have time to pick her up. I knew she'd come here first and I was happy. Her plane would be here sometime this morning. We could hopefully work on Mom's defense before she got here. Then we could work on the funeral arrangements when she arrived. When her brother and sister heard Dad died at the hands of Mom, they were probably ready to call the Klan. To this day I believed they are, or were at one time, members of the KKK. I hoped Aunt Libby would be able to keep them under control through the service. They hated my mother. Thank goodness they were older; hopefully, they wouldn't try to retaliate physically. I wasn't holding my breath.

Not only did we have to pull the funeral together, we had to explain two new grown twin boys, his sons.

David arrived at the house fifteen minutes before ten. Jerome explained in detail what happened in the house the day our father was shot. It was a struggle. It was an accident but by Jaden leaving the scene and Mom not cooperating with the police, this was not an open and shut case.

Mom slept late. I finally heard her fussing around in her room. I didn't know how much more she could take. We had to confront her. She had to admit the truth about Jaden's presence at the house. I knew the guilt she felt for never going after her sons was overwhelming. Succumbing to Dad's demands became her way of life.

The doorbell rang at exactly ten. The beats from my heart were so strong I thought everyone could see the vibrations coming from my chest. I suddenly became queasy, sick with anticipation. I'd waited seemingly forever to have my mom and brothers all together – though, this wasn't the reunion I'd been dreaming of. I ran to the door and flung it open.

"Hey, Princess, how are you? Are you okay, sweetie?" Aunt Libby had on dark sunglasses which was unusual for her. When she removed them, I knew why – to mask her puffy eyes. Her face was clean from her normal blush, mascara, and lipstick. Dragging herself through the door, Aunt Libby swung her arms around me. "Are you all right?"

"Fine, Aunt Libby." I turned away from the opened door to guide her into the family room where Jerome and David were still talking.

"Brittney." Nerves jumped all over my body when I heard a voice from the front door. I turned to see Jaden standing at the door. I was speechless. I grabbed his arm and hugged him.

"I didn't get a chance to hug you last night. Thank you for coming."

"No problem. It's all good. I think we were all in a state of shock last night anyway."

"Come on in so I can introduce you to..."

Before I could complete my sentence, Aunt Libby blurted out, "Oh My God! You're one of the twins." She clasped her hands over her mouth and started sobbing. Before I could say another word, Jerome walked into the foyer to see what the uproar was about.

"What's going on?" Jerome asked.

Aunt Libby grabbed her chest but couldn't speak. I thought she was going to stroke out. "Aunt Libby, these are your nephews Jaden and Jerome. We have a lot to tell you but right now we need you to come into the family room so we can get Mom out here."

"She hasn't seen them yet?" She held her arms out to both of them. "Come here." She wrapped her big jelly arms around them at the same time.

"She has seen them but not together. We'll explain everything in a minute." I looked at Jerome. "Take them into the family room to meet David while I get Mom."

I stood at the bedroom door. I could hear the shower running. I opened the door and sat on the bed until Mom finished her shower.

"Oh, good morning, Princess, I didn't know you were waiting for me."

"Good morning, Mom. I came to see how you were and to tell you David is here. We have to discuss your case this morning."

"No. I want to work on the funeral arrangements this morning. We can worry about that case stuff later. I have time." She shrugged her shoulders casually.

"We'll work on your case this morning. David is already here and so is Aunt Libby."

"Libby is here? Why didn't you tell me earlier? Did she meet Jerome?" She walked over and flopped on the bed beside me, gleaming with joy.

"Yes, she met Jerome. You need to get dressed and come out right away."

"Oh everyone must think I'm such an awful mother."

"Mom, you don't need to be in here worrying about what anybody thinks right now. You could possibly go to jail for the rest of your life. What people think should be the last thing on your mind. Please get dressed." Her distraught look calmed my anger. It reminded me of her fragile state. She quickly put on her jeans and a T-shirt.

"Let's go, missy, I'm ready." She threw her arms up as if she were about to give the performance of a lifetime.

I didn't know if I'd done the right thing by not telling her Jaden was here also, and we knew the truth. Instead, I allowed my mother to walk into a room and have her past hit her dead in the face. As soon as she turned right from the hall entering into the family room, she saw Jaden and Jerome sitting together on the sofa.

She covered her face and fell to her knees weeping and shaking her head. "No. No." I dropped down beside her, trying to hold her up. I couldn't so I just held her.

Jerome and Jaden rushed to her, kneeling at her side. Her three children were with her, comforting her. She looked up at each of us then turned back to Jaden. "Why are you here? You have to go. Please, don't stay here." She cried.

"Come on, Mom. Get up. We have to talk." I said. Her sons helped lift her from the floor, escorted her to the sofa, and each son sat at her side. I wanted to take a picture, but this was no Kodak moment. We needed to get to business. "Mom, we found Jaden last night. He told us what really happened."

She abruptly turned to Jaden. "No. I told you I'd take care of everything. Don't say anything else." Then she looked at David. "He's confused. He wasn't there. You're my lawyer and I demand you not accept his statement."

"Mrs. Adams, I know you want to protect your son, but we have to give this information to the District Attorney's Office to clear you. This was still an accident, so we can probably get both of you cleared of this crime."

Mom cried. "Probably? You don't understand. I've never been there for my sons and now he's in this trouble all because of me. I won't let him go to jail for one night over this. I can't depend on a 'probably.' You need to guarantee me Jaden will not be in any trouble over this or I'll get on that stand and testify under oath that he's lying." She faced Jaden. "I've lived my life. I don't know what kind of life you have, if you have a family or not. We didn't get a chance to talk, but you deserve to have a happy life. You mentioned you'd been in trouble and no one would believe you. Now you have more family. You have a sister and your brother. Maybe they can help you get your life together. This was still an accident either way, so why do they need to know you were there? No one needs to know."

Jerome took her hand. "Mom." I was shocked to hear someone other than myself call her mom. Hearing her son call her mom, she laughed and cried at the same time. "How do you think Brittney and I found out Jaden was there? Someone saw him before the shooting. Think how easy it was for us to find him. The detectives will do the same. It's only a matter of time until they find him and bring him in for questioning. It would be better if we go to them with this information and cut a deal." He held his hands up in retreat. "A deal where no one does any jail time."

Aunt Libby sat in the recliner as quiet as a mouse. I'd almost forgotten she was there. It was hot. Her face was drenched with sweat and tears. She finally spoke out. "I'm only getting bits of information here, but am I hearing correctly? You both shot Richard?"

"Aunt Libby, it was an accident." I kneeled down at the foot of the chair. "Dad came home and found Mom and Jaden in the bedroom, jumped to the wrong conclusion, and pulled his gun out. Jaden and Mom struggled trying to explain to Dad he was their son and the gun went off." She sat silently for a few minutes, shaking her head back and forth. "That stupid jealous, stubborn fool got hisself shot due to that ugly mean streak of his. Oh, Lord, why couldn't he just listen?" She pulled her heavy body out of the chair. "I have to go out and get some air." She took a couple of steps towards Mom. "He did love you. He was just confused about a lot of things and carried a lot of pain and guilt around that haunted him continuously. Sometimes I think he was brainwashed by our father. He was his only example of how to be a man. He was my dad, too, but he was a sorry excuse for a husband and father. I'll call Herbert, Jr. and Nelda to see when they're coming."

I was thrilled I didn't have to talk to my uncle Herbert or my aunt Nelda. They carried the same idiotic ideas as Grandpa Adams, even in this present day. I hadn't seen them since I was a little girl so I was sure they weren't as vocal as they used to be with their racist views, but Aunt Libby told me they still felt the same way.

"I need to make that call now." David watched Jerome, Jaden, and Mom. He then focused only on Jaden. "Are you okay with that?" Jaden nodded yes.

Mom leaned into his shoulder and cried. Jaden wrapped his arm around her. "It's going to be fine. We have to trust Jerome." Jaden watched Jerome worriedly but with trust in his eyes.

"Make the call," Jerome said. My brothers seemed to have a natural bond, although they'd just met for the first time in thirty-two years. Mom's genes were definitely dominate in the three of us.

The days had flown by since the truth had been revealed at our little family reunion. Aunt Libby and Mom worked together yesterday making all of the phone calls while I worked with the funeral home making all of the arrangements. In a couple of days, we would face the real judge and jury, Dad's family. Herbert, Jr. and Nelda had already told Aunt Libby they didn't want to see Mom at the funeral.

The audacity of them to come here and make demands on who should or should not attend my father's funeral. They were the ones that had disowned him. If anyone should be banned from the funeral, it should be them. I was ready for a fight. I found myself getting more and more anxious as the date got closer.

Chapter Twenty-Five

The evening of the viewing, Aunt Libby and Mom stirred around in the kitchen. Family and friends had been coming over to pay their respects and more would follow after the viewing.

"I thought people were supposed to come over after the funeral, not the viewing?"

Mom said, "Sometimes people like to stop by and see the family after the viewing as well. Besides, your Dad was a lieutenant and in the department for over thirty years. We want to be prepared for whatever."

A lot of people had already been by to give their condolences in the past few days. The rumors started to fly that Mom and Jaden were getting away with murder. We tried to keep Mom away from the media. David had finally made a comment to the press that it was a horrible accident and Mom would eventually be cleared of all charges. One of my father's first cousins came sashaying in the house as if she owned the place. I recognized her from the few family photos we had. She didn't care for my mother either, but she stayed in touch with Dad. She looked around with her nose held high. I jumped up from my seat in the living room and plowed towards her before she could get to Mom in the kitchen.

"Hello. I'm Brittney, Richard's daughter." I reached my hand out to shake hers. She gave me a puny fake grin and hesitantly shook my hand.

"Hi. I'm Victoria, your dad and I are first cousins."

"Yes, I know. I've seen your picture and think I remember visiting you as a child."

"Wow you have a very good memory if you remember that...you were very young the last time I saw you. How are you doing? How are you holding up? This must be so hard on you."

"Yes. It's a difficult time for all of us, but we're managing."

Victoria leaned in and whispered, "I mean with your mom being the one that killed your father. You must be livid. I mean mad as hell at..."

"It was an accident. An accident my father himself caused. My mother has been through a nightmare over this, so I'd appreciate it if you didn't mention anything like that again while you're in my home." I gave her an iced stare that expressed "if you speak another word, I'll cut out your freakin' tongue."

She took a step back and smirked. "I'll just go over and say hello to your mother and to Cousin Libby, then be on my way."

I was still staring without a blink. "You do that." She pranced her way to the kitchen and gave my mom a shy hug and then gave Aunt Libby a big bear hug as if she'd lost her husband of thirty plus years. Well, it was Aunt Libby's brother, so I guess that was all I could expect out of the wench. At least she had the decency to come and give her condolences to the family. The other hicks wouldn't even come or call. I didn't trust her so I stayed close to Mom while she was there.

Jerome and Jaden had moved from the living room to the kitchen and family room. Jerome watched me watching her and immediately went on guard as well. I had made it very clear to Jerome and Jaden how Dad's side of the family was so there'd be no surprises for them. We were all in protection mode for Mom.

Victoria spotted Jerome and Jaden entering the room. "Oh, hello. I'm Victoria, Richard's cousin." She extended her hand. "And you are?"

"I'm Jerome. Nice to meet you."

"I'm Jaden."

"You two are twins?" They were identical with Jaden's clean shave and hair cut. Jaden was still skinnier with a sunken face.

"Yes," they said in unison.

"How cute. That must have been fun growing up together. Did you guys play tricks on your teachers?"

"No," Jerome said.

Victoria seemed taken aback by Jerome's abrupt response. She turned back towards Mom. "Are these your nephews, Marilyn?"

"No. They're my brothers, her sons," I quickly announced.

Victoria stretched her eyes while leaning back. "Excuse me?" Her mouth was still hanging open and her eyes shifted from Jerome back to Jaden.

"Don't have a cow, Victoria. These are Richard and Marilyn's sons. They were given away for adoption at birth. Now roll your tongue back in your mouth." Aunt Libby had an uppity southern accent. "Now give your cousins a good-ol' 'welcome to the family' hug."

Victoria closed her mouth and followed instructions and gave Jerome and Jaden each a feeble hug. Then she turned to us and gave us a mournful good-bye.

We all laughed when she left. We decided if anyone else asked, which we knew several people would, we wouldn't go into details about how or why they were given up for adoption. We'd just keep it simple. All agreed.

"How did you like your pity hug from your cousin, man?" Jerome joked with Jaden.

Jaden grinned. "She coulda kept that."

The wake was from five to seven in the evening. Me, Mom, Jaden, and Jerome arrived fifteen minutes before five and planned to stay until seven fifteen. Aunt Libby left at six thirty to go back to the house in case anyone showed up there before seven. The air-conditioning in the funeral parlor was blasting, so many left to hang outside to thaw out.

My father laid in the casket looking like a distinguished gentleman, in his Department Class A uniform with his Lieutenant's bars shining on his collar and his hat resting over his hands just above waist level. He was still quite handsome for sixty. I watched my mom shed a few tears now and then, but I didn't cry. As a matter of fact, I hadn't cried at all. At least not for him; I wasn't sure why.

My father had touched many lives. Old and young, women and men paid their respects. I found myself surprised by all of the nice things so many people had to say about him. Then again that's what people do. They say nice things when you're dead. Despite the kind of person you were while living.

Just minutes before seven, Herbert, Jr. and Nelda walked in with cousin Victoria. The Snyders, the last family to leave, said their good-byes at the door when Nelda waltzed in glaring at Mom then rolling her eyes up in the back of her head. We all noticed it but pretended we didn't.

When the Snyders left, Mom took a deep lengthy breath and then turned to face her enemies. Only Jerome, Jaden, Mom, Herbert, Jr., Nelda, Victoria, and I remained in the room. There was a row of chairs in front of the casket. Mom walked over and sat down, watching them. We followed closely behind her but stood on the side. Herbert, Jr. stood over Dad shaking his head while one of his arms wrapped around Nelda. Victoria positioned herself next to

Nelda but slightly turned so she could view the casket and the rest of the room at the same time.

Minutes later, Herbert, Jr. turned and walked towards Mom. "I guess you couldn't rest until you put my brother six feet under. Could ya?"

I wanted to curse his butt out but I didn't want to escalate the situation, especially there. So far this was mild compared to what I expected. Mom leaned back and crossed her legs, clutched her hands in her lap, and gave him the coldest, darkest, fearless stare but never said a word.

Nelda leaned in inches from Mom's face. "If you think you're gonna git away with murdarin' my brotha, you're sadly mistakin', lady. I won't rest until you're in jail."

By this time my blood was boiling. Nelda was too close for comfort. I said, in the calmest coolest voice I could conjure up, "Get out of my mother's face, Nelda, before I give you and your clan a reason to put me in jail."

"I think you guys need to leave," Jerome spoke in a professional authoritative voice.

"So you're the smart-ass kid? Daddy was right. He said you guys would end up turning on your own dad."

Everyone exchanged perplexing looks. Herbert, Jr. knew Grandpa Adams had convinced Dad to give Jerome and Jaden up for adoption? Even the wicked witch of the east, Nelda, was caught off guard.

"You knew about this?" Nelda muttered.

"Yes. Daddy didn't want you and the other ladies to know. You know how soft and simple you are when it comes to this kinda stuff. But ya see he was right. Look at 'em standin', there supportin' the woman that killed their father. I already dun talked to that D.A. and I know one of you fellas was in on the murda. You killed your own dad. I think it was you." He pointed at Jaden. "You can't tell me this was some accident. You dun this on purpose. Come hell or high water, I'm gonna gitcha for killin' my brotha."

Mom had sat there through all that gibberish as still as a cactus standing in the midst of the desert. She finally stood. "My, oh my, what love you're showing for your brother now that's he's gone. Where was all this love for him when he reached out to you when your parents turned their backs on him? Where was all this concern when he longed to talk to his big brother when he reached milestones in his life he wanted to share with his family? Where was this so-called love when Brittney was born and he sent you pictures of his little girl he was so proud of, only to receive the letters sent back unopened?" Mom looked at Nelda. "Where was all this love and concern then?" Mom chuckled. "Now that he's gone you have the audaciousness to show up here and allow the words 'my brother' to slide off of your tongues as if you even understood the meaning of the word." Mom turned to me. "I'm ready to leave now." With that, she walked away. I watched her strut towards the door with pride. My mom was back.

I smiled at Herbert, Jr. and his little gang. "Um, I guess you guys heard that. Now tomorrow at the funeral, I want you all to behave yourself like you've had some sort of home training, okay?" Then I walked out proudly with my mom and my twin brothers at our sides.

Epilogue

I wish I could have been a fly on the wall to see David and Jerome work the deal. They spent several hours preparing Jaden and Mom's defense. The D.A.'s Office determined it was an accident but Jaden got one year probation for fleeing the scene of a crime. Mom didn't get any jail time or probation. They agreed due to the situation, they both acted in self-defense.

Jerome stayed with me for another two weeks after the funeral. We saw Jaden several times each week, catching up and being supportive to him. He took us to meet his adoptive mother. She extended a warm welcome to us and was happy to see Jaden finally at peace with himself. He couldn't figure out why he was always acting out when he had a mother that loved him. Something just gnawed at him. He couldn't put his finger on it. Jerome helped Jaden find a night school for welding. He enrolled for the fall semester. He went from a world of hopelessness to a world of hope in a matter of weeks.

Jerome and I met with Angela on several occasions, and she finally agreed to talk to Anthony. A lot of her anger was at herself and her mom for allowing her to get into this situation. She and Anthony became friends again. She was sixteen. He was nineteen. Both had gotten drunk and had sex. She changed her mind in the midst of everything. I decided, whether wrong or right, to stay out of that. Anthony was very supportive. He enrolled in Los Angeles City College not far from his house. Angela was talking to her mom again but decided she wanted to remain at Ebony Eyes' Home for Girls until she had the baby.

Matthew and I were closer than I ever expected. I was also doing some soul searching to see why I even entertained the thought he was with me because of my mixed heritage. I realized I had a few things to work out.

Jerome's last day before returning to Maryland, we all met at my house for dinner. Aunt Libby remained in town for another three weeks to continue offering support to the family. Finally I had the Kodak moments I had hoped for, my twin brothers with my mom. Deep down, I knew my father would never be part of this picture, a loving family. If my father wouldn't have been so afraid of the unknown, I believe he could have loved his black sons the same way he loved me and Mom.

Mom put the house up for sale that she and dad lived in for over twenty-five years. She said there were too many horrible memories there.

When Mom, Aunt Libby, and I were alone in the kitchen, I asked Mom if Dad ever hit her. "No," she quickly responded. Aunt Libby and I quickly exchanged a baffled look. I'm not sure if I believed her and from the look Aunt Libby gave, I'm not sure she believed her or if she knew Mom was lying. I guess I'll never know.

Discussion Points

1. Was Brittney too quick to think her father was racist versus just a man mimicking his father of how to be the man of the house?

2. After years of not going after her sons, do you think Marilyn cared more about keeping her husband happy rather than going against his extreme wishes?

3. Was Marilyn in denial of being an abused woman? Do you or do you know someone who is verbally abused but does not think her husband/boyfriend is that bad?

4. Although Brittney didn't seem to have mental issues from being bi-racial, do you think she had regrets of being the product of an interr2acial couple?

5. Do you think Brittney tried extremely hard to only relate to her Black heritage and wanted to deny her White heritage?

6. Do you think Matthew should have backed off completely from his relationship with Brittney after her radical outburst when he confessed his love to her?

7. Do you believe a racist person can fall in love with someone of another race?

8. Can you understand Jerome's faith in God when he had only been in the Church as a very young boy?

9. Do you think Jaden's parents regretted adopting him after he began a life of criminal activity?

10. Can you relate Jerome and Jaden's story to someone you know? Do you know someone who was abused as a child, but beat the odds and became successful?

11. Do you think Jerome mentoring young men was therapy for his tragic past?

12. What did you like or dislike about this book?

ISBN:978-0-9828670-0-6

CPSIA information can be obtained at www.ICGtesting.com
Printed in the USA
237537LV00002B/66/P

9 780982 867006